Ripper Pass

In the dusty streets of Miller's Pass a killer stalks women of the night. Hiding in shadows, vanishing in the light of dawn, he frenziedly butchers with impunity. Ex-manhunter Jim Hannigan and his lovely partner are called in, but this killer is unlike any Hannigan has ever previously encountered.

This figure out-manoeuvres and taunts the law, leaving a trail bathed in scarlet. Is he outlaw, ghost or one of the town's bizarre players? With his partner's life threatened, Hannigan must race against time before more victims are added to the tally of a truly fearsome murderer.

Ripper Pass

Lance Howard

A Black Horse Western

ROBERT HALE · LONDON

ISBN-10: 0-7090-7943-5
ISBN-13: 978-0-7090-7943-9

Robert Hale Limited
Clerkenwell House
Clerkenwell Green
London EC1R 0HT

For Tannenbaum

Typeset by Derek Doyle & Associates, Shaw Heath
Printed and bound in Great Britain by
Antony Rowe Limited, Wiltshire

CHAPTER ONE

July 22

Annie O'Dell wasn't having a particularly good night and she knew for certain it wouldn't get a damn sight better if Pruitt caught her in this condition. Staggering, she nearly tripped over something non-existent on the sawdust-covered saloon floor. Her head danced and the Durham-clouded room two-stepped before her vision. The reek of rotgut and smoke, cheap perfume too heavily applied, and sweat clawed at her senses. Her belly somersaulting, she struggled to keep from bringing up her last meal. What the devil good would she be to any fella if her cherry bodice was a-stink with her own innards?

Not that she was much damn good anyway. Pruitt called her the ugliest whore in the county. Popular opinion and too many mornings staring into a small silver mirror – the only gift she'd ever received and kept from her departed ma, may her soul burn in everlasting hell – agreed.

Cowboys from local ranches, passing-through tinhorns and a gaggle of Miller Pass's vow-breaking husbands crammed the tables in Pruitt's saloon. Whoops howled from players slapping down winning hands, un-Christian words spat from losers' mouths, a few punctuated with threats aimed at cheating opponents. Any possible violence, however, met with quick stifling from Jack Pruitt. The saloon owner perched behind the bar, dark eyes surveying the crowd, mostly focusing on his girls. His hand remained only inches away from a shotgun beneath the counter at any given time or the Bowie sheathed at his waist.

Annie cast him a glance once her head stopped two-stepping, skin crawling as his gaze pinned her, promising that if she didn't bring in more money tonight she'd be in for another whupping. Her belly swirled again with the notion; she still had bruises from the last encounter.

The piano-player began pounding away at keys, no ear for tune or finesse with musical phrasing. The sound jangled her nerves, making her head want to whirl again. Goddammit, she had to lay off the laudanum, at least this early in the evening. But she couldn't stop herself, could she? The more Jack beat her the more she wanted – needed – to drown the pain and forget the fact that even as a whore she was an utter failure. 'No damn good for anything', her ma used to say. It had taken only twenty-two years for Annie to figure out the bitch was right.

Damn her. Damn Jack. Damn Miller's Pass. No way out, not for her, not for any of the girls in this place. Least, not till the Good Lord came calling. Judas Priest, what was she thinking? Lord wanted nothing to do with her or her kind. Elsewise she wouldn't be beggin' for two bits every night from filthy, dung-stinking cowboys. Even that new marshal hadn't improved Miller's Pass any. He'd been here a week and what had he done? Nothing for her kind, that was for damn sure.

Annie spat, a reflexive gesture, one she couldn't stop in time. Her spittle landed on a cowboy's shirt sleeve and he glared up at her. His face, beard-peppered and looking for all the world like a chicken had danced over it, twisted into a scowl.

'Christamighty, missy, you best tell me you didn't just spit on me!' He jumped out of his seat. The cowboy next to him, a slight man with watery eyes, placed a hand on his forearm.

'Now, Billy, ain't the first time a lady's spat on you, is it?' A cocky smile filtered onto the second cowboy's face, the man too drunk to realize his co-worker wasn't finding the incident half as funny as he did.

Billy snapped a short punch that mangled the smaller cowboy's nose. The injured man jumped back in his seat and grabbed his bloodied nose, wheezing. 'Goddamn, Billy, I was just funnin' ya!'

Billy glared at the man, wiped the blood from his knuckles on his trousers. 'You best keep your goddamn mouth shut, Drew, 'fore I add your teeth to the list of things broken on your face.' His gaze jumped back to Annie, who was praying the man had taken out his wrath on his partner and would let her alone.

' 'Sides,' Billy said, 'this ain't no lady. This here is Miller's Pass's ugliest goddamn whore. How much you get for a turn, you homely mule?'

The words cut. They shouldn't have. She should have been used to it and she'd been called far worse. She wanted to claw his eyes out, screech at him that men didn't goddamn care so much about looks when their peckers was doin' the talking. But she couldn't. If she did Jack would beat her even harder.

'P-please . . .' Her words trickled out, barely more than a whisper. 'Please, don't . . .'

Billy's face tightened with a sadistic look she'd only

7

witnessed on two men, Jack and the man her ma said was her father, a no-good owlhoot who only came 'round when he needed his bell rung and couldn't find no one else to do it.

Billy grabbed her suddenly, jerking her close. One hand groped at her rump, the other snatched a fistful of her mousy hair and yanked her head back. His gaze swept over her thin lips and too large nose, sallow skin and the deep, dark pockets beneath her watery, bloodshot eyes. 'Galldamn, but you sure are uglier close up, ain't ya? Not even worth two bits. Hell, skinny little ass on you like that, I wouldn't even take it free.'

Her lips quivered, but anger boiled in her veins and she suddenly drew closer to him, forcing her mouth an inch from his. He grinned, thinking she was trying to use her sex to persuade him to go easy on her, but the moment she felt his grip slacken she sank her teeth into his bottom lip.

He bellowed and shoved her away, hand going to his gashed lip. 'Goddamn whore, she done bit my lip clean off!'

Annie spat again, this time a mix of saliva, blood and a piece of his flesh. She glared, heart pounding, sweat trickling between her bosoms.

'Stay the hell away from me, you no-good sheep-poker. Just stay the hell away from me!' She spewed the words with as much venom as she could muster, then a sobering chill washed through her innards at the thought of what Jack was going to do to her for treating one of his customers this way.

Billy's eyes widened, a blaze of anger sweeping over them. 'You goddamn mattress warmer, I'm—'

His words ended in a choked squawk. Her gaze focused

8

behind the cowboy, then clouded with fear. She hadn't seen Pruitt step from behind the bar and thread his way through the tables. A burly man, fully capable of bending a horseshoe bare-handed, he moved quickly for a fella his size and no one in town dared get on his bad side. Billy had forgotten the house rules, and no matter what Jack would do to her for her transgression, no one damaged his merchandise, except him.

In one fluid move Jack had grabbed Billy's wrist, which had come up in a fist intended for Annie's face, with one hand and plucked the Bowie from his belt with the other. A brittle snap sounded. Billy let out a bleat like a branded calf. His wrist bones had buckled under Jack's crushing grip. The saloon-owner's knifehand swept up, jamming the blade to Billy's throat. The edge penetrated a fraction, drawing a trickle of blood. Billy's eyes darted, sweat trickling from his brow, mouth clamping shut.

'I told you we got rules in this place.' Jack's voice came through clenched teeth. 'Don't touch the ladies 'less you intend paying for 'em and don't fight in my bar.'

Billy murmured something unintelligible.

'Don't think I heard you . . .' Jack withdrew the knife a hair.

'S-sorry, Jack, didn't mean nothin' by it. Was just funnin', that's all.'

'You get your fun some other way, you sonofabitch, or next time I'll send your head home by its ownself.'

Billy tried to nod, but couldn't move much against the blade. 'S-sure, Jack. Sure thing.'

Jack released him, flinging him towards the door. Billy glanced back at Annie, eyes promising something, but avoided looking at the bar-owner. He staggered towards the batwings. His partner, still clutching his broken nose, slid his chair back and darted for the door.

The barroom had gone dead silent the moment Jack grabbed Billy. Things returned to normal with a few murmurs building into loud voices, then to its regular cacophony a moment later.

Jack's gaze settled on Annie as he sheathed the knife. 'You get the hell upstairs and sober up, you stupid waste. I catch you on that laudanum again this early and you'll wish to goddamn hell you'd swallowed enough to take you to your Maker, hear me?'

She nodded, trembling now, lips quivering. She wiped a hand across her mouth, swiping away Billy's blood. 'Y-yes, Jack. I won't do it no more, I promise.'

'I'll deal with you later for what just happened. Don't think you're gettin' off easy.'

A bolt of terror sizzled through her and she almost lost her balance. She had all she could do to nod, then stagger towards the stairway at the back of the room. She fell against the banister, gripping it so she wouldn't collapse, nails gouging into the pitted wood. She stared up into the darkness, then back towards the barroom proper, seeing Jack watching her as he headed back behind the bar. His eyes narrowed and she quickly looked away.

Straightening, she half-pulled herself, half-stumbled up the stairs. The clamor of the barroom dwindled behind her, wavering in and out. For a moment she wasn't entirely sure she hadn't started to lose consciousness. She reckoned only her deathgrip on the banister kept her from tumbling back down the stairs.

As if in a trance, she reached the top and stared into the darkness of the hallway.

A buzz of something rippled through her belly, not fear exactly, but something close. Why was the hallway dark?

They always left two wall lanterns turned low so they could see when they led men up here to the rooms where they plied their trade. Yet the hallway was black as coal.

A niggling voice deep in Annie O'Dell's mind told her she should turn around and take her chances with Jack in the bar, instead of going forward into the darkness to her room. She assured herself it was simply the laudanum wearing off. Nothing more. She'd walked this hallway a hundred times and nothing was any different tonight, except for the lanterns being extinguished.

'You're not a little 'un afeared of the dark, are you, Annie?' she chided herself, not sure whether she had spoken the words or merely voiced them in her mind. A moment later, Annie O'Dell took a step into the darkness for not the first time in her life.

She reached out, palms flat, finding a wall. Her vision began to adjust to the darkness, allowing her to pick out dim outlines of walls and doors.

With each step her heart thudded a beat faster for no reason she could figure. A feeling came with it, one that settled like serpents slithering over one another in the pit of her stomach.

'Christ . . .' she whispered, hands now trembling. It was the laudanum wearing off, she told herself, half-believing it. Another swig and she'd be good as new.

But Jack would kill her if she didn't lay off that stuff.

No, she couldn't face another night of rejection without it, she couldn't face the looks and taunts, the hurt.

Christamighty, that's the ugliest damn little girl I ever seen!

Her father had said that on her seventh birthday. Right before her mother stuck a knife between his slats. The words had burned into her mind for all time, because even though her mother had made him pay for it Annie knew he was right. She saw it frozen in her mother's eyes every time she looked at her. Annie O'Dell, the gal with the face demons chuckled at and angels never looked upon.

'You ain't ugly,' her ma had said, a half-moment before the trap-door shuddered open and her neck snapped for the crime of murder.

But even then her eyes said different.

A scuffing sound tore Annie from her dark memories and she gasped. The slithering snake feeling swelled from her belly to invade her entire body. She stared into the darkness, frozen. A dim outline met her startled gaze, a deeper blackness against the gloom. A figure, a man.

She caught a scream just before it escaped her lips, swallowed it. A match flared, its glare stinging in its suddenness, hurting her eyes. Squinting, she caught a glimpse of a face before the flame died, and some of her fear trickled away. But not all of it.

'Christ, you damn near scared half my life off me!' Her voice jittered; she fought to control it.

The man said nothing, simply tossed the burnt-out match to the threadbare carpet. His fingers dug into a pocket of his trousers; a moment later she heard a dull plink ring out just in front of her high-laced boots. She knelt, feeling for what she knew was a coin, finding it. Straightening, she held the coin up before her eyes, certain it was gold. Greed overwhelmed any remaining apprehension.

'This—'

'Double-eagle.' The man's voice came low, muffled.

'Why you talkin' funny?' She peered into the darkness, having a hard time distinguishing his form.

'How would it look if we were overheard?' He took a

12

step forward, towards a door, a door that led to her room.

'No fella's ever paid me this much.' A note of incredulity and doubt laced her tone.

'Perhaps they didn't need you for as long I wish.' Something in his voice should have warned her, brought back the fear. Perhaps in some distant part of her numbed mind it did. But greed and a perverted sense of gratitude overruled any qualms she might have heeded.

She stumbled forward as he shoved open her door and let out a giggle that matched the tone of her features. She'd never had a pretty laugh, the way the other girls did. It sounded more like that mule Billy had called her. But for now she didn't care. For once in her life Annie O'Dell was going to be a queen for the night, and she would never tell that bastard of a barkeep just how much she'd earned to play the part.

He closed the door behind her as she stepped past him. Staggering to her nightstand, she located a lucifer and fired the lantern.

'Turn it low.' The man kept back in the shadows by the door. 'I don't require much light.'

She glanced back at him, shrugged, turned the flame lower, then replaced the chimney. For a moment she didn't turn. She merely stared at the small hand mirror on the stand. Picking it up, she gazed at its silver filigree, now as tarnished as she. Her gaze drifted to her reflected features, but this time a soft smile touched her lips, instead of one of disgust. This time she was something, worth a double eagle like the high-class gals in Dodge or some such place. This time Annie O'Dell was traveling Hansom.

The feeling lasted but an instant.

'W-what?' she whispered, belly plunging.

A glint had flashed across the mirror. Before she realized what caused it, he grabbed a handful of her hair and jerked her head back; her gaze swept across the darkened ceiling. The mirror dropped from her hand, clinking on the floor. The man stepped forward, forcing her back against his chest, a boot-heel coming down atop the mirror, shattering the glass.

Pain. Only an instant, but deep, burning. Then warm liquid that seemed almost to freeze as it flowed from a deep gash across her throat down her bosom. She gurgled something, the sound lost as darkness swarmed in from the corners of her mind.

July 30

Elizabeth McBride hated these humid hot nights in Colorado. Somehow they made her feel even dirtier than she normally did, and that wasn't an easy mark to beat. Sweat zigzagged down her face and dribbled onto her chest. The top of her peek-a-boo blouse was soaked and most of her small bosom was on display for anyone who happened to pass her on the darkened street. She didn't care. She was used to displaying what she had, which, truth be told, wasn't near as much as she wanted.

Not that she wanted for customers; that pleased Jack no end, saved her from the beatings most of the other whores got. She was prettier than them. God had bestowed upon her face the tilt of an angel's and blessed her body with a true gift when it came to pleasing menfolk.

Shadows swayed across the boardwalk ahead and she stopped, a sound sending a small shiver skittling through her, despite the heat. Hanging lanterns provided enough light to see her way as she headed towards the boarding house where she lived, but somehow the watery heat made everything seem sinister tonight. Maybe it was just her annoyance with it, or maybe the fact she'd inhaled that powder her last fella had paid her with, but shapes appeared deformed, reaching . . . *menacing*.

'Get hold of yourself,' she whispered, wrapping her arms about herself. The streets were empty, a listless breeze stirring dirt and swaying hanging signs until they sounded like coffins opening. She'd made the walk a hundred times before. What should be so different about this night?

That girl. That ugly one who used to work at the Pruitt, the one they'd found butchered in her room upstairs. That had set all their nerves on edge. She'd never seen the like. She'd been the one to discover the body and it was a horror that would live in her mind till her dyin' day. The way that poor girl had been all cut up like that . . .

No, it was her own damn fault. A whore had to learn to take care of herself. Only the ones who did survived and that woman had . . .

Had what?

Whatever she'd hoped to convince herself with evaporated like mist under a brassy sunrise. She couldn't rightly blame that dead girl. The powder was just pricking at her paranoia, dredging up the horrible sight in her mind. Hell, that was why she'd started taking the stuff in the first place, to forget, but nothing erased that night from her mind. Now it was only making things worse. But she could no longer stop herself from using it. Something about it gripped her innards, made her want more every time it wore off. And if she didn't get it within a few days she got sick, heaved her guts and shook like a kitten in the snow. She craved it, the way she craved men, no matter how dirty it made her feel.

15

A contradiction, that's what she was. Born and bred into a fine family, proper schoolin', then suddenly everything just went to hell past her thirteenth birthday. 'Fore she knew it she was trying things no decent girl ever had the right to try, and not long after that she couldn't stop.

She'd always been that way. It shouldn't have surprised her, that wild streak, the tendency towards addiction. She knew better, but the need to experience overrode common sense.

And now she had fallen to this, a new low. Becoming more pathetic by the day.

Liz McBride forced herself to take a step forward, swallowing at the lump of vague fear now lodged in her throat. Just the powder, she fought to convince herself; that's all it was.

Her high-laced boots scuffed against the dust-coated boards as her steps quickened. The sound was like demons chortling.

Her heart picked up a beat, for no real reason other than the powder's effects. That happened often now, the rapid heart beat, the sweating, then nausea. She had more in her room, if only she could get to it before things went totally awry.

Elizabeth . . .

She stopped, a small sound of fright escaping her lips. A chill wriggled up her spine, though sweat poured down her chest.

'Who is it?' Her voice came unsteady, breathy. She had heard her name called, by a muffled low voice. Hadn't she?

Christ, she suddenly wasn't certain.

'I said, who's there?' She stared at the darkness ahead, buttery lanternlight chased away by gobbling shadows.

16

No sound, save for the signs creaking and a scratchy hush as grit skittered across the boardwalk.

She took another step, heart now in her throat.

You're scarin' yourself for no reason. But the blood-drenched image of the dead woman flooded her mind, making her shudder. She stumbled, boot toe hooking on a protruding board. She flung out her hands as the boardwalk rushed up to meet her. Skin scraped from her palms and her elbows buckled. She hit the boards face first, the impact only partly blunted by her hands.

'Oh, Jesus H!' She pushed herself up into a sitting position, wiping her bleeding palms on her skirt, then pulling her peek-a-boo blouse back up over her now exposed bosom. Her ankle screamed with pain; she'd twisted it going down. Forcing herself to her feet, she shouted, 'Goddammit!' frustration overriding the ambiguous fear. She staggered along the boardwalk, the sense of foreboding from a moment ago forgotten as her ankle throbbed, bringing tears to her eyes.

Then it was back. Suddenly. Completely, like a wave of black chilled water poured over her soul. An alley stood to her right. She had just begun to pass before it when something grabbed her arm. Fingers dug deep into her flesh and she cried out in pain and fright.

Darkness swallowed her as someone dragged her deeper into the alley. A silent black world all around her, she could feel him there more than see him. A wall hit her face as he slammed her front-to against the shiplap siding of a building. A hand groped over her back while the other forced her face against the wall.

'Pathetic little whore . . .' A whisper reached her ear; hot breath slithered against her cheek. Terror surged from deep within her.

'Please, please . . . don't . . .'

A whispered laugh, then he yanked her face away from the wall and his arm hooked about her waist. Her feet lifted off the ground. He slammed her to the dirt floor of the alley, on her back. Breath exploded from her lungs, stars burst before her eyes. A weight pressed against her, his knee jammed to her chest. She wanted to plead for her life, but the words never left her mouth. Fingers dug into her face, forcing her chin up. She heard the terrifying sound of a knife sliding against leather.

Elizabeth McBride said a silent prayer, knowing for certain now that Annie O'Dell had done nothing to deserve her fate. She hoped the Good Lord wouldn't hold her sins against her.

An instant later, fire sizzled across her throat and the darkness of the alleyway grew infinitely more intense.

August 6

'If I give you any more I won't have enough to pay my rent and keep Jack from beatin' the hell outa me!' Polly Maybrick, eyes pleading, pulled up her bodice, then climbed from the bed in her boarding-house room. 'Bad enough I'm gonna be late back to the saloon and Jack'll have my ass.'

'Everyone in this goddamn town's had your ass, Polly.' The man who said it swung his legs out of bed and reached for his britches, which were slung over the back of a rickety chair against the wall. His dark face carried that sadistic grin he always had when he made jokes at her expense. She hated that look; sometimes she hated him, but couldn't stop herself from obliging whenever he took to being randy as a bull scenting a cow in season. She tried to turn away but heard him utter a grunt that told her she'd damn well better look him in the eye when he was talking. She knew the consequences of ignoring his order.

'Jesus, Aaron, I ain't heard no complaints from you 'bout it.' She said it before she could stop herself. She did that sometimes. Well, often, more often than she knew was healthy, considering the two men she answered to, her lover, Aaron Darkwolf, and Jack Pruitt, enjoyed beating their women. She hoped he was drunk enough to let it pass.

His eyes glittered in the low lanternlight, narrowing as they sought to focus on her. He stood, lips drawing tight. He grabbed his Bowie knife from the night table and he slid it into a sheath thonged to his belt loops. 'You best not be sassin' me, you no-good saddle. You know I won't take none of that from you. Folks in this town might think they can treat an Injun that way, but you ain't on that list.'

She forced back a shudder. Her trembling hand went to the strawberry-blonde curl corkscrewing along the left side of her face, twisting it. Her eyelids fluttered as she searched her mind for some lie to tell him, finding none. Just as well. It would show on her face. Polly Maybrick had her share of talents, but lying had never been one of them.

'Please, I have to pay Jack tonight. I come up short you know what he'll do to me.'

A sneer filtered across Aaron Darkwolf's lips and he followed it with a disgusted sound. 'That sonofabitch'll get what's coming to him one of these days.'

She almost laughed; a giggle slipped out. 'Who's gonna give it to him? Ain't a fella in this town, even that marshal, who'll stand up to him. And I don't see you—'

A backhanded fist made her swallow the rest of her words. She couldn't get out of the way in time. A shock of pain rattled her teeth. Blood spurted from her mashed lip

19

and she let out a bleat, then stumbled backwards. Legs losing all strength, she went down, back hitting a wall, sliding part of the way. She gazed up at him, vision clearing after a moment.

As she dragged a hand across her bleeding lip she felt her temper surge, though she knew it was a mistake to defy him. 'You ain't never lifted a finger against him. You can damn well hit a girl but you're nothin' more than a scared little rabbit when it comes to someone who can hit back.' It wasn't true and she knew it. She'd seen him nearly a kill a man once for calling him a half-breed. But when it came to Pruitt he always backed down. She reckoned it had more to do with the money she brought in than fear.

'Why, you no-good—' He took a step towards her, the muscles across his bare chest rippling with tension as both hands curled into fists.

Her fingers darted for the derringer in her skirt pocket. She pulled it on him, her hand shaking as she aimed at his chest. He stopped, a spiteful smile on his lips. 'I swear, you hit me again I'll kill you.' Her words quivered, and she knew the lie was plain.

He laughed, his teeth biting into his lower lip. His head lifted and he stared at some spot on the wall. 'Hell, you know you won't shoot me, Polly. Don't have it in you. I could beat you within an inch of your life, just the way Jack does, and you'd still be that needy little girl who always comes runnin' back, tail 'tween her legs. That's just the way you are. You can't help it. It's the only reason I don't leave your sorry ass to the drunks in this town.'

Her hand trembled the more as she sought to pull the trigger. It should have been easy. His gloating face, his arrogant voice, should have made the flick of her finger against the trigger the simplest thing in the world.

Her hand lowered. She tucked the derringer back into her skirt. She pushed herself to her feet as tears ran from her eyes and blood poured from her lips. She reached into her pocket again and drew out the few coins she had left and hurled them at him. They rebounded from his chest and landed on the floor. His smile widened.

'See?' His dark eyes focused on her. 'It's always the same, Polly. Why do you insist on going through this every goddamn time?'

'You bastard . . .' The words came low, steeped in disgust at herself for being so weak.

He nodded. 'That's Injun bastard, or ain't this town made that clear to you yet?' He grabbed his shirt from the chair and shrugged into it.

She let out a shrieked curse and grabbed either side of her hair, pulling, out of anger and frustration that she could hardly bear. He laughed and she whirled, flinging open the door and running out into the hall. She heard the heavy thud of his footsteps start after her.

Her heart was pounding with impotent fury. She grabbed the edges of her worn skirt and ran down the dimly lit hall to the door that led to the street. She hurled it open and plunged out into the warm night, tears clouding her vision. Everything appeared blurry, streaks of shadow and amber. Her feet clomped along the boardwalk as she headed for the saloon, oblivious to the few passersby she crashed into.

You're gonna leave that sonofabitch! she told herself. *You have to or he'll kill you one of these days.*

No one would have considered her anything more than a cheap whore, but, Christamighty, she had some speck of pride left, didn't she? She couldn't let him keep hurting her, keep stealing what she earned. She couldn't.

21

But she would. And she knew it. She would always run back to him, no matter how bad he treated her, no matter how much of her earnings he took. No matter how many fragments of her pride he crushed beneath his hatred for everyone white, including his own personal whore. Because she couldn't stop herself. She didn't know what sick twist of her soul sent her back to him night after night, month after month, beating after beating. She wished, to a Lord who never listened, that she did know.

She stopped, collapsing against a support beam for a wooden awning, gasping, heart pounding so hard she thought it would burst through her chest. Why couldn't she just die, right here, right now, and never have to face her pitiful excuse for a life again? She leaned over the rail, vomiting into the dust, mostly from fear, but a little from her disgust with herself.

The sound of a footfall came the moment her retching stopped.

She drew the back of her hand across her lips, wiping away the remnants of her supper, and looked back, seeing no one. But he was there, somewhere, she knew it, had heard him. He was toying with her, warning her he was close. He'd done it before, played cruel games with her, terrifying her until she felt paralyzed with fear. It was part of his pleasure, a way to take out his rage at this town.

The passers-by had vanished into buildings, leaving the street deserted. Shadows bunched in corners and side-streets, lanternlight anemic, somehow utterly cold.

She pushed herself away from the beam, stumbled along the boardwalk.

Another footfall, purposely loud.

She whirled. 'I know you're there, Aaron!' The sound of her shout echoed in the silence. 'I know you're there.

Please, no games tonight. Jack's gonna be pissed enough 'cause I'm so late.'

Did she hear a whispered laugh? Eyes narrowing, she stared along the boardwalk, seeing no one. But he was there; she felt him watching her. This game was different somehow, it occurred to her. He wasn't usually so subtle. A dark suspicion coiled in her belly and the memory of two other women from the saloon invaded her thoughts, two other women who'd been . . .

'No . . .' Her voice was barely audible. 'Not that . . .'

A burst of panic rattling her, she whirled and ran for the saloon. She chanced a backward glance, praying that this once Aaron would just step out into the light and allay her fears. But she saw no one.

She twisted her head forward again, then stopped dead, slamming into a dark figure blocking her path. Too frightened to scream, she struggled to push away from the man but he clamped a hand over her mouth and wrapped the other about her back. As he dragged her into a side street, she kicked at his shins and knees, tried to claw at his face, pry his hand from her mouth.

He hoisted her off her feet, hurled her away from him. She slammed into the dirt, on her side, pain skewering her hip and a rib cracking with a brittle sound. Groaning, she saw his black figure loom over her. He grasped her arms, lifted her, then carried her to a small courtyard surrounded by a wrought-iron fence.

He kicked open the gate and took her deep into the courtyard, then hurled her against a wall. The impact knocked the air from her lungs and sent renewed pain through her cracked rib. She toppled forward, hitting the ground again face first. Small sounds of agony came from her lips, lasting only a moment, because the figure

23

grabbed her arms and flipped her onto her back. A sudden shocking burning at her throat told her she would never again have to worry about anyone beating her. In the last instant before death stilled her mind, Polly Maybrick felt something she never felt before: no fear, no regret for a life wasted; she felt free.

CHAPTER TWO

There were two things Jim Hannigan wasn't looking forward to: risking Tootie's life on another case and revealing just who had hired him to look into the trouble in Miller's Pass. Well, he had to admit, maybe the second part brought a hint of callow expectation when he considered her jealous reaction. Course, with a woman like her it was like as not to backfire on him.

He shot a sideways glance at the young woman riding beside him, the rough motion of the horse beneath her counterpointing the serene look on her Mex-spiced features. Something pinched in his belly. That look was a contradiction, and he knew it. She always got that look right before she started questioning him about something he felt damned uncomfortable answering. Her mahogany doe eyes stared at the sunlit trail ahead, but schemes played behind them. It didn't take a mind reader to know what she was thinking. Suppressing a groan, he dreaded the conversation he'd known was coming since the day in Revelation Pass when he'd figured on riding off without her. It had been only a matter of time.

Another thought struck him: she was lovely in the early morning sunlight. Her long legs, glimpses of which flashed from beneath her riding skirt, her straight black hair shining almost blue in the honey sunshine, all made him feel things inside he reckoned he had never felt. But with those feelings came uneasiness. Would this case be their last? What if he couldn't save her the next time her life was threatened?

It was a risk that Tootie del Pelado took willingly, but one he took seriously. He couldn't lose her. The feelings were strengthening, growing unmanageable, at points endangering his own life, because they occupied far too much of his concentration. But the only other choice was leaving her, and he'd discovered in Revelation Pass that that wasn't an option as he'd thought it to be.

He sighed, sweat trickling down his face and chest. Jim Hannigan was a man who'd seen much violence in his life; fate had branded it upon his very soul. The thought of that violence destroying the woman next to him made him want to scream his insides out.

Well, like she said, the choice was hers. She risked herself for her work before he came along and would after he was gone, if that was what he chose.

But that made it no easier to swallow.

As his gaze focused straight ahead his thoughts wandered, but not for long.

'You got somethin' on your mind . . .' She said it without turning towards him, voice a bit harder than normal. It wasn't a question.

'Reckon not.'

'You're a poor liar.'

'Heard tell there's folks who'd debate you on that.'

'They'd be wrong.' She glanced at him, lips firm, face serious. 'Don't think I didn't see you lookin' my way from the corner of your eye, either.'

He shrugged, annoyance filtering into his veins. She was too damn perceptive for his own good. He wasn't used to folks reading him so well, and she was better than anyone had a right to be. That meant he was likely exposing himself more. That meant he was losing the edge he'd worked so hard to hone since the day his ma . . .

'Don't bother denying it,' she said. 'You know better.'

'Wasn't planning to.' He had been, but he wouldn't admit it. The roan beneath him nickered, as if laughing. He was starting to wonder whether even his horse was figuring him out.

'Like I said, you're a poor liar.'

'Had your bag sent on ahead. It'll be at the hotel when we arrive. You're registered under the Hannah Garret name.'

She let out a small laugh, letting him know she was on to him. Changing the subject was something he'd never been particularly graceful at, and this attempt was clumsier than most. Fact was, Jim Hannigan couldn't even count the social skills he'd never bothered to learn. A man who men hired for vengeance didn't need those skills. He needed cold nerve and a well-oiled gun.

A frustrated expression leaked onto his lined face. He swore she smiled at that, but the expression vanished too quickly for him to be certain.

'You still haven't told me what this case involves or who hired you.' She was playing along for the moment, lulling him, but relief filled him all the same.

'Three bargirls got themselves murdered.'

She nodded, glancing at him, then back to the trail. To either side the woodland lay thick with aspen and ash, fir and spruce, gnarly brush. Low hills rose to the west and the forest sloped gently to the east. Morning birds twittered and the occasional scurrying of woodland animals reached his ears. The day was warming fast and had become bright enough to cause his habitual squint to kick in. The scents of late-summer flowers and horse lather filled his nostrils, along with a fleeting whiff of her perfume, which smelled like something close to heaven.

After a moment she spoke again: 'How they get killed?'

'Cut to pieces, from what I hear tell. Like nothing ever seen in these parts, 'cept maybe after a Comanche raid.'

'How'd you find out?'

'Got a letter.' He hoped she wouldn't focus on the fact that he was being purposely vague, and more on the particulars of the case.

'These girls who got killed, anything I should know about them?'

'Such as?' He hoped the relief in his voice at her not zeroing in on the specifics of the letter didn't show. At the same time a measure of disappointment pricked his hide because she didn't ask.

Jesus, Hannigan, what the hell's wrong with you? Can't have it both ways . . .

'Such as, they related in any way, anything in common?'

'Other than all being whores, not to my knowledge. Just three random killings.'

'Where?'

'Place called Miller's Pass.'

'Never heard of it.'

'Reckon after three killings it'll be on the map soon enough.'

She went silent for a moment. He braced himself; that was usually a bad sign.

'I best see if I can get into the local saloon. Best place to start.'

He cringed. 'Christ, you know I don't like that.'

She smiled, didn't she? It came and went in a blink, but he knew she got some sort of kick out of pulling his string. 'Afraid I might take a likin' to it?'

He sighed. 'You know that ain't what I mean.'

She let out an easy laugh. 'I know. I can take care of myself. You know that. We've been over it a hundred times.'

He glanced at her, his face tightening with worry he couldn't bury. 'An' likely we'll go over it a hundred more. That won't change things. This one's too dangerous.'

'Everything we do is dangerous. You damn near got yourself killed on our last case.' A glaze of anger came with the words and he knew he'd be better off just dropping it before they got into another feud.

'Three women are dead. Best we make no mistakes this time . . .' He let it go at that and she gave a small nod.

'Who sent you this letter?'

His belly cinched and a muscle ticked near his eye. He knew it was coming, knew he'd have to deal with it once they reached town – if she let it go that long. The sense of devilish satisfaction he'd expected over telling her was suddenly nowhere near as strong as he thought it would be. 'W-What?'

'I asked who sent it? Father of one of the girls, beau, someone else?'

'They were whores.'

'Reckon you said that already. That's why I'm askin'. Ain't likely too many folk'd care what happened to them.'

'Reckon you're right.'

'So which one?'

'Which one what?'

'Father or beau?' She was toying with him again, but a

29

note of suspicion came with it.

'Neither, exactly.' His voice dropped to a mutter. He drew a deep breath of warm air and held it, waiting for the other boot to drop.

'This person who sent it, wouldn't be a gal by any chance?'

He squirmed in his saddle, his hands tightening on the reins. 'Reckon it might have been.'

She nodded. Her tongue poked at her lower lip and her eyes narrowed. 'I see. Ain't like you.'

'What ain't?'

'To go runnin' off on a case at the request of some gal. Usually hire out for a lot of money. Can't imagine anyone would care enough to pay us much for three murdered bargirls.'

'This one's . . .' He searched for a way to put it, coming up short.

'This one isn't paying, is it?'

'Reckon not. That mean I can persuade you to turn back?' He should have known better than to poke a sleeping badger at this juncture, but times were many when his mouth worked before his good judgement when it came to Angela del Pelado.

Her voice got a cold edge. 'So who is she?'

'Who's who?'

'You know what I'm askin'.'

He shifted in his saddle. Any satisfaction he'd thought he'd feel at seeing her jealous evaporated completely now. Some expectations just didn't deliver on their promise and this was one of them.

'Her name's Catherine Tretlow.'

She nodded, an expression that carried with it an unspoken: *I'm not satisfied with that answer.*

'You know her?' she asked.

'Reckon.'

'Know her well?'

'You jealous?' Sometimes he just couldn't stop himself from digging the hole deeper.

'You really want to take that trail?' She glared at him and he might well have shrunk to a size small enough to crawl under his saddle.

His voice lowered. 'I knew her a long time ago.'

'How well you know her?'

He shrugged. 'Well enough, I reckon.'

'That isn't an answer.'

'Best one I got.' He went silent, uncomfortable enough not to look at her, though he could feel her gaze riveted on him. Explaining Catherine held all the appeal of falling naked into a winter creek.

They rode in silence for another mile, the sun skirting higher, chasing away morning shadows. The gentle clopping of the horses' hoofs against the hardpack wasn't as comforting to him as it usually was. The situation presented a more acute danger directly to Tootie than their previous cases. Normally he went in with a notion of just whom he was tracking, commonly at the request of another who'd lost someone dear. This wasn't the same. It was no simple bank robber, outlaw, or kidnapper. He had no idea who the killer was or why he was killing, and the target was women of the line, the very role Tootie planned to portray. Add to that the woman who'd summoned him here . . .

A memory wormed its way from the depths of his mind, an unpleasant recollection of the last time he had seen Catherine. Before it could form completely, Tootie interrupted.

31

'We have to talk about it. You know that, don't you?' She glanced at him but he remained focused on the trail ahead.

'About what?'

She sighed. 'You were going to abandon me in Revelation Pass.'

'I would have come back.' He reckoned it was the first honest thing he'd said to her about their relationship and he didn't quite understand why. He usually buried his responses in sarcasm, or avoided them completely.

Her mahogany eyes widened, as if she were shocked she hadn't been forced to pry the answer out of him. 'You expect me to believe that?' No accusation in her voice, no spite, only the need for a truthful answer.

'Said yourself, I'm a poor liar.'

'Why?'

Christ, couldn't she just let it go at that? Why did women need complicated answers to everything, anyhow?

The woodland thinned and roughly a mile ahead the outlines of buildings came into view. He felt immensely thankful for it, and reined up, lifting his head a notch as he peered into the distance.

'That's our town. We best split here. You ride in first, get settled. I'll come in in about an hour. I want to scout the outskirts first.'

She just peered at him, lips tight with an expression that said the discussion was far from over. She reined around and heeled her horse into a ground-eating clip towards Miller's Pass.

He watched her shrink to a speck and drew a deep breath. He wondered if this case would be the one where one of them went down. He prayed that if that happened it would be him, and that she would give up this life they led should that be the case.

'Yah!' He sent his horse into a gallop, veering off-trail to skirt the town. All the thinking and fretting in the world wouldn't change what was to be. For now, he had a job to do and he'd best get to it.

Bertrand Mitre lowered the spyglass and tucked it into the leather pouch hanging from his left side. He'd seen enough. His dark eyes narrowed and he ran a beefy hand over his stubbly chin as a grim smile inched on to his lips.

'Hannigan . . .' he whispered, edging back behind a large aspen, so he wouldn't be spotted by chance.

Satisfaction swelled within Bertrand Mitre for the first time in seven years. That was how long it had taken him to escape that hell hole of a jail where Hannigan had left him to rot. It hadn't been hard tracking the manhunter to this place. Not hard at all. Man with that sort of reputation made the papers, likely more than he would have wished, and the sonofabitch had acquaintances everywhere. Bertrand had only needed to kill two of them to get a line on the manhunter's base of operations, plus of course the Nancy-boy secretary working there the day Mitre scouted the place for a sign of his quarry. The secretary had literally screamed Hannigan's destination once the blade tip wedged beneath his gumline.

The girl riding with the manhunter was a surprise, but a welcome one. He'd figure out a way to use her in his revenge somehow.

'Soon, you bastard . . .' he muttered. 'You'll pay for what you did to me.'

Bertrand Mitre wasn't a large man, barely over five feet eight inches, but he was nearly as wide. He spent his time in jail working his muscles until they swelled at the arms of his shirt and gave him a strength that made him capable of grabbing a neck in one hand and crushing it until cartilage and bone snapped. He'd killed his prison guard that way. It had been one rare occasion when he'd felt satisfied using anything other than the Arkansas toothpick at his waist for murder.

Funny thing was, Hannigan had brought him in for bank robbery. The manhunter hadn't even known about the string of butchered men and women Mitre had left across Montana and Wyoming, just because he was right fond of watching folks die before he took all their valuables. He reckoned it was his part Nez Percé blood that made him hunger for the feel of steel slicing through white flesh and clean bone. Or maybe it was just plain meanness. He'd never really cared which. Had Hannigan known this the day he brought him in, Bertrand Mitre would have hanged long before now.

But he didn't know. He didn't know the man he'd left to rot had escaped and he didn't know that that man had waited, marking the days, until he could chase him down like the dog he was and slice him into little pieces. Bertrand Mitre never forgot a debt and outstanding payment accrued a hell of an interest.

But not yet, no, not yet. The girl made revenge all the sweeter. Obviously she meant something to Hannigan. He would do her first, maybe in front of Hannigan, so he could watch the life bleed out of her. It was only a question of timing, isolating her, then making sure Hannigan knew just enough to lead him to the scene at the appropriate moment.

The matter had to be handled cunningly. Hannigan was damn fast and damn accurate with that piece of his, crafty when it came to tracking. He was blessed with that manhunter's sixth sense, and likely that had been the only thing that had saved him from Mitre getting the jump on him and slicing his throat the first time they met. That or pure dumb luck.

With the back of his hand he pushed up his battered felt hat and mopped a line of sweat from his furrowed brow, then spat. His left hand went to the hilt of his Arkansas toothpick.

'Soon, my friend, uh? Very soon, indeed.'

CHAPTER THREE

Miller's Pass was a lattice-work of streets. Laid out more like an Eastern city, it boasted a narrow main street with evenly spaced side avenues, wrought-iron-railed court-yards and squares. The hardpacked earth was fairly level but the conglomeration of structures boasted styles from adobe to brick, shiplap to shack, as if someone had given plenty of thought to planning the layout but not a notion to building symmetry. The sun glared from windows sport-ing gilded lettering, sparkled from troughs. Hannigan noted the usual array of businesses: mercantile, general store, saloon, marshal's office, hotel, gunsmith, sawbones. Hardly appeared a place for the type of murders Catherine had described. Her letter had related a sinister, death-stalked town, with a vicious killer the likes of which no one had ever encountered.

He slowed his mount, guiding it along the main street, his gaze curious, picking out every detail, searching for any possible sign of threat. Folks moved about the board-walks carefree enough. Of course, the murders had been confined to whores, so they probably reckoned they had little to be concerned over. That could change in a heart-beat. Anyone brutal enough to murder three women in such a way might well explore his options – unless he had a specific reason for targeting women of the line.

Questioning the townsfolk might prove dicey at this juncture, with only whores endangered. Whores' acquaintances would likely be confined to men, some of them possibly husbands, so he'd exercise prudence, at least till he had reason not to.

His gaze settled on the Pruitt saloon, a handful of buildings away to his left. He'd find Catherine there, according to her letter. But why? What had turned her from the girl he knew into a woman who sold herself for money? She was the last person from whom he would have expected that. Fact, by now, he would have figured on her being some high-falutin society fella's wife.

Unless you left her on that road . . .

Christamighty, you arrogant sonofabitch! he chastised himself. That's taking guilt to its extreme, isn't it?

Maybe. But a wormy notion wriggling in his mind made him wonder. They hadn't parted on the best of terms, so it had surprised him more than a little when he got her note. He was the last person on earth he would have expected her to turn to.

But Catherine always did have a soft spot for those less fortunate and a way of doing the unexpected. That she would be concerned over the deaths of three women no one likely gave a damn about, as well as the possible threat to others, was the one thing that didn't surprise him.

He located a livery stable and made arrangements to board his horse and tack. Having paid for two weeks in advance, he slung his saddle-bags over a shoulder and headed for the hotel. He'd made the reservations for himself when he made Tootie's. It would look a little peculiar, them both coming in within such a short span of each other, but he doubted it would pose a problem, at least at first. No one knew them here and Catherine had never met Tootie.

A pang of apprehension stabbed his belly at the thought of their meeting. Catherine was going to be hard to explain, though he reckoned he owed Tootie no explanation.

Hell, you don't. You can't keep denying your feelings for her. You best make your past an open book if you expect her to stick around much longer.

The way hers was open to him?

He grunted, gave a small shake of his head. He reckoned he didn't know a hell of a lot about her past yet, but he got the notion she kept it close to her vest till such time as he decided to share his with her. Wasn't fair to expect more than that. Secrets were a part of what his life had become, who he was. Same for her.

Christ, for now, he'd be satisfied just knowing how she managed to get into locked rooms so easy.

He stopped before the Dusty Gull Hotel, drawing a breath and setting himself. He'd only just arrived and already his nerves had started to crawl, as if the darkness that hung over the serenity of this place were burrowing into his composure. The sensation washed over him with unexpected strength, and he realized he'd felt it briefly on the trail, too, as if someone were watching him, observing his every move. It wasn't possible, he reckoned. No one knew they were here except his secretary back in Denver.

Forcing the feeling away, he entered the hotel. The place appeared clean, with sparse furnishings and worn carpeting. He crossed the lobby to the front desk. A small man in a visor looked up as he approached and nodded a greeting.

'Morning to ya, gent,' the clerk said. 'Lookin' for a room?'

'Already registered. Hannigan's the name.'

The clerk perused his ledger and nodded, jutting a bony finger at the book. 'Ah, yes, there it is. Jim Hannigan. Room 19, just like you asked for. Faces the street. You plan on a two-week stay?'

'I'll pay you for that. I leave early any extra's yours.'

'Very good, sir, very good.' A smile flittered onto the clerk's long face. He reached behind him to a pegged board and grabbed a key, then slid it across the counter. Hannigan signed the book after the clerk turned it his way, then counted off enough greenbacks for two weeks.

'Ah, there was the matter of a woman?' the clerk started and Hannigan nodded. He tossed a few more bills onto the counter.

'You don't know we're together . . .' He said it low, but it came with enough authority to make the man blink.

The clerk nodded like a jackrabbit. 'And if she should leave early?'

'Remainder's yours.'

'Ah, very good, very good. Will there be anything else? If one woman ain't enough . . .'

Hannigan eyed the man as he snapped up the key. He wanted to say one woman was plenty when it came to Tootie, but refrained. 'Maybe you can provide me with some information.' He'd figured on getting the full story from Catherine first, but you fished in the pond that looked promising.

'I'm right connected.'

Hannigan figured he would be. The little clerk's eager eyes had nosy scribbled all over them. 'Heard 'bout some killin's 'round these parts.'

The clerk shook his head, 'Oh, no, sir, nothing for you to worry about. Your young lady's quite safe here.'

Hannigan nodded. 'I'm interested in the murders. What do you know about them?'

The clerk shrugged. 'Three whores, no one'll miss them. Awful thing, though. Heard tell it was the most gruesome thing ever to hit Colorado Territory. Fact, never heard of nothing like it back East, neither.'

'You got details with that?'

'I got a touchy stomach. Ain't interested in knowing the particulars. You might want to try the doc, though. Heard he examined one or two of 'em. He don't like workin' on whores but the marshal insisted.'

'That the sawbones I noticed a bit down to the left as I rode in?'

'Only one we got. They didn't even bury the bodies in the cemetery. Just hauled them out to the pigs on Tucker's farm.'

Hannigan's belly pinched. 'Damn disrespectful, ain't it?'

The clerk's brow lifted. 'Just whores. Pigs gotta eat.'

Hannigan eyed the man with a measure of disgust, then headed for a stairway running along the back wall. He'd gotten all he needed from the clerk for now. Tracking a whore killer was not going to be easy in a town that didn't give a damn about a human life, no matter how lowly some considered it.

He located his room and settled in, flinging his saddle-bags over a bed post and eyeing the place. The room was small, with striped blue-and-white wallpaper, a bureau holding a porcelain pitcher and basin filled with luke-warm water. The bed boasted clean sheets and a rickety chair stood in a corner, a night table with a lantern flanked the bed. He went to the window, gazed out into the street. Noon brought more folks into the open, the majority heading for a café a few blocks down. He could see the newspaper office and saloon from here, but not the sawbones's office.

He moved away from the window, deciding on a quick visit to the sawbones before meeting with Catherine come evening.

Tootie would be settled in her room by now, which was one door down, as per his reservation. She was better off there for the time being. He wished she would keep to her Hannah Garret disguise but saw damn little chance of it. She would be too eager to go right to the source, and he bet getting a look at Catherine would likely add to her motivation.

With a defeated sigh, he went back downstairs and left the hotel.

The sawbones resided only a few doors down. A hanging sign that had seen better days said: DOCTOR T. FRANCIS. He entered the office and stepped into a small reception room filled with wooden chairs and a small desk. No one was about but he noticed an open door leading to the examination room. He doffed his Stetson and crossed the reception area to the door, pausing in the entry when he spotted a man with a long flowing mustache and ruddy complexion poised over a microscope.

The room held an examination table in the center, two deep leather chairs and a cabinet with glass doors that held numerous brown and blue bottles filled with myriad elixirs. A counter ran along the west wall. Hannigan's gaze froze there. If his belly had rebelled with the hotel clerk's news of pig feeding, it completely revolted now. Lined along the counter were a number of jars, each filled with murky liquid and various fleshy objects. Hannigan had little knowledge of what went inside the human body and preferred to keep it that way, but it was plain where the objects had come from. An odor pervaded the room that did little to alleviate his queasiness. Sour, biting at his nostrils, the bouquet of some sort of preservative, he guessed.

As his gaze jerked from the containers he realized that the doctor had turned to stare at him. The man rose from his stool. He stood about five-ten, stocky, with spectacles that made his eyes look far bigger than they were. A heavy gold ring adorned his left index finger.

'Anatomical specimens.' The man's voice showed a measure of annoyance, but also a hint of amusement at the distaste registered on Hannigan's features. 'I've collected them from a number of deceased individuals. Matrices of young women, a few kidneys, a liver, spleen. Fascinating, don't you think?'

Hannigan stepped into the room. 'Reckon I should ask why you'd have such things . . .'

'Who are you, sir? What do you want here?' The doctor's annoyance magnified.

'Name's Jim Hannigan. I'm here in an official capacity.'

'That so?' Did he hear mocking in the man's voice? He was damn near certain he did. The doctor moved to a table that held a number of instruments, among them a razor-edged scalpel. He selected the scalpel, then went to one of the jars on the counter and returned with it to his microscope. 'I see no badge and you do not appear to be a lawman. We have a marshal, so I can't imagine what you might be.'

'I'm not a lawman. I work for hire.'

Francis nodded, mustache bobbing. 'I see.' He twisted

the lid from the jar and with tongs lifted the specimen from within. Hannigan wasn't quite sure what the organ was and had no desire to find out. 'I take it you're here about the murders, then? Someone hired you to discover who's doing away with Miller's Pass's less illustrious citizens?' After setting the organ on the table, he sliced off a section of the tissue, then replaced the remainder in the jar and screwed on the lid. He located a small glass slide, placed the excised part on the flat surface and slid it beneath the microscope.

'Close enough for intents.' Hannigan said. 'Three women, all killed horribly, I hear tell.'

The doctor nodded, peering into the lens of his scope. 'Disease, Mr Hannigan – and, by the way, I've heard the name. Seems you got some worthless author building you into some kind of hero. I don't rightly find killers to be heroes, myself.' Hannigan damn well didn't like the judgement in the man's tone, but he wasn't here to justify his career.

'Disease?' The odor in the room seemed suddenly overpowering, whittling away at his composure.

'Disease. You asked why I should have such a thing as these specimens. That's the reason. The human body can tell us everything about its maladies, if we know where to look. I look at the tissues, seek the answers in the very material of life.'

'Any of these *materials* from the murdered girls?'

The doctor looked back to him and gave a small smile, then shrugged. 'They were just whores, Mr Hannigan. A blight on the West. Nobody cares what happens to them. I wouldn't have even given them a second thought had our marshal not forced me to examine them.'

Hannigan nodded, folded his arms. 'But you did examine them?'

Francis nodded, straightened and turned to the manhunter. 'I did. All of them had their throats sliced, the cut running left to right, an incision commencing at roughly two inches in a straight line below the angle of the jaw. The cut deepened as it went, carving through cartilage and severing the carotid artery. The women bled to death before the more sordid cuts were applied.'

Hannigan's eyes narrowed. 'More sordid cuts?'

A peculiar twinkle of fascination showed on the doctor's face. 'Quite a sight, really. Their stomachs were slashed open, but the killer didn't stop there. He removed some of their innards and arranged them nicely about their bellies, at least with two of them, like an artist might arrange objects for a painting. The third wasn't as bad, but I reckon he must have been interrupted.' The doctor went on to describe the rest of the mutilations with almost a reverence for the killer's work that struck Hannigan as damn morbid.

After the doctor finished, Hannigan shook his head. 'Christ, sounds like you're describing some sort of monster, not a man.'

'Hardly, Mr Hannigan. Why, there are tales of such things amongst the Comanche, are there not? Did you know they cut their victims into pieces to prevent them from seeking revenge in the next life?'

'You saying these killings look like the work of Indians? No Comanche in this area that I'm aware of.'

'Perhaps not, but there's a fella in town who's part Crow. Maybe you should discuss these murders with him.'

'Who is he?'

'His name's Aaron Darkwolf. Animal skinner by trade, drunk by profession. Marshal hauled him in once or twice for causing disturbances.'

'What reason would he have to murder three whores?'

'Perhaps you should ask him that.'

Hannigan raised an eyebrow. 'I got the notion you think you've got the case solved.' The doctor appeared a bit too eager to palm off the crimes on some local half-breed to Hannigan's way of thinking. The man's prejudices were scrawled plainly across his words.

'I'm a country doctor, Mr Hannigan. Not a detective. That's not for me to decide.'

'Every country doc in these parts keep jars of anatomical specimens?'

The sawbones studied him, as if trying to discern whether a deeper meaning lay behind the question. 'If that's all you require from me, sir, I have work to continue.' A tone of dismissal laced his voice. Hannigan might have been more inclined to press the doctor further had it not been for a desire to escape the sickening odor, but he would hold off for the time being. He wasn't entirely satisfied with the sawbones's answers. Add that to the man's obvious dislike for women of the line and Indians and he reckoned the doc would warrant a return visit soon enough. He put the half-breed down for a parley as well.

'Reckon I got what I came for.' He placed his Stetson on his head and left the room, the doctor staring after him, eyes narrowing.

Tootie del Pelado heaved the portmanteau onto the bed in her hotel room, then flipped open the compartments. She'd retrieved the bag from the weasely little clerk after fending off his not-so-subtle advances. Hannigan wouldn't be long behind her and she wanted to get onto business before he got a chance to try to talk her out of it.

If he thought he was going to keep her out of the saloon after telling her about this Catherine woman, he had another think coming. Any trepidation she might have felt about compromising her modesty again vanished the moment he'd mentioned the woman who hired him – a woman from his past.

Who was she? Who was she really? Obviously Hannigan knew her from somewhere. Had they been lovers? Simply friends? What was so special about her that he'd taken this case gratis so fast?

You're being far too jealous, she chastised herself. She bet Hannigan knew it, too. She finally gotten a measure of honest emotion out of him and he'd managed to turn the tables before she could capitalize on it. That annoyed her. Bad enough that little stunt he'd pulled before they left Revelation Pass. She had fully intended to make him pay for that for a good two weeks more, but this changed things.

You can't go on this way, a voice inside warned her. You can't keep feeling things for a man who won't let you close. It'll tear your heart out bit by bit.

She'd told herself she'd give him time, wait until he was ready, but each day near him made that more difficult. What if he never got ready? What if he never gave anything more than he gave now? Could she accept that?

She doubted it. Patience wasn't exactly her strong suit. Besides, she had too much respect for herself.

You don't really know why he acts that way, she reminded herself. She had seen his feelings, though he tried to disguise them. He could keep them out of his words but not out of his eyes. Some sort of pain got in the way, something from his past that stopped him from letting himself trust her with his heart. Yet the way he worried over her on cases, the way he made mistakes now because his mind was preoccupied with concern over her welfare . . . that said something, didn't it?

But did it say enough?

It had to, at least for now.

On the other hand, this Catherine woman was fair game. Maybe she knew something about his past, something that would provide her with a way in.

What if they were . . .

She didn't want to think about that. It would only complicate things more. And with a murderer running loose, she needed to be on her game. She was putting herself directly at risk this time, in taking on the part of a bargirl. Maybe Hannigan was right and the role was a mistake . . .

Why was she suddenly feeling unsure of herself? Were her feelings affecting her more than she realized?

It was this life, she told herself. It was wearing on her, whittling her down sliver by sliver. And it'd keep wearing her down until there was nothing left, unless she could ground herself before it did. But that depended partly on Jim Hannigan, didn't it? Alone, things went on the way they always had, more pieces of her soul flecking off. At least until a mistake got her killed. But with him . . . well, together they completed each other, formed an impenetrable shield against the erosion this way of life worked on a body.

Sighing, she lifted a blue sateen bodice from the portmanteau. After setting it out on the bed, she pulled out a skirt and frilly undergarments. Five minutes later, she'd changed from riding clothes into the whore's get-up. She located a small make-up case in the bag and propped the mirror attached to the interior flap against a pillow so she could see her face. She paused, studying the dark half-circles beneath her eyes, the small lines around her mouth and eyes. The strain was showing, ageing her prematurely. Maybe that was a good thing where this disguise was concerned, but not a good thing for her peace of mind and vanity.

She twisted the cap off a tin and daubed coral onto her cheeks, over-applying so it looked tawdry. Next she smeared kohl above her eyes, then slid two silver pins along either side of her head to pull back a layer of hair and give her a double parting.

After she finished, she fished a derringer from the portmanteau, tucked the weapon between her breasts, then closed the case and slid it beneath the bed. She reckoned she'd used enough make-up to differentiate herself from Hannah Garret, since she was forgoing the blonde wig this time.

She padded to her door, opened it a crack and peered out into the hallway. Hannigan was nowhere in sight. She slipped from her room, went down the stairs and scooted across the lobby to the door. She saw the clerk staring at her in a peculiar way. She smiled, holding out her hands, palms up.

'Got paid for the whole night,' she said and he nodded, obviously wondering just how she'd managed to get in without him seeing her but, she hoped, not pondering about her resemblance to the woman he'd checked in a short while before. ' 'Bye, sugar . . .' She giggled and stepped outside.

She made a beeline for the saloon, wanting to remain out in broad daylight no longer than necessary. Normally she would have waited until dusk for such an excursion, but her curiosity over Catherine had gotten the better of her.

She scolded herself for being over-eager, knowing that that sort of thing led to mistakes, but this once she reckoned she'd get away with it.

On reaching the saloon she pushed through the batwings. Only a handful of bargirls polishing glasses or leaning on the counter occupied the barroom, along with a husky man standing behind the bar. He shot her a look that made her want to take a step back. She wasn't often intimidated, but a cruelty glinted in the man's eyes that was nearly palpable. A wave of black threat radiated from the way he stood, chest out, mouth tilted at a hostile angle. She trusted her intuition about folks, and right now it raised the hairs on the back of her neck, warned her this man was one to watch closely, make no mistakes with.

'What the hell you want?' His tone backed up the impression, cold, demanding, a fella used to giving orders and seeing them obeyed without hesitation.

She forced her composure to return. 'Why, sugar, I came in here lookin' for a job. Heard this was the best place in town.'

'It's the only place in town. I see to that.' He stepped out from behind the counter and came towards her, gaze raking her, though the one thing missing from it was lust. 'I s'pose you'll do. A bit scrawny for my tastes.'

She wouldn't tell him how relieved that made her feel. Had he touched her or wanted any kind of initiation, she would have had to kick his saddle-bags to the next county. She cleared her throat. 'Name's Tootie. Reckon I don't have to tell you how I got the name.'

He nodded. 'You're jest lucky we got vacancies.'

The reference to the murdered girls was just the opening she needed. 'Why ever for? You don't mean gals would want to go elsewhere?' The sugar in her voice made her sick. The more she was around this man the more she felt some sort of darkness coming off him. She suppressed a shiver.

'Murdered. Those bitches deserved what they got. They was always stepping out of line and I don't tolerate none of that.' His voice showed no sympathy, no compassion. He didn't care and that was that.

'Killed? My gawd, how's such a thing happen in a fine little town like this? Who would do such a thing?'

He laughed, as unpleasant a sound as any she'd ever heard. 'Somebody who don't take bullflop from women. You got any notions of not doing what you're told you best watch the same thing don't happen to you.'

She wasn't sure whether it was a threat or some kind of perverted jest. This was going to be trouble. She had always been adept at maneuvering around doing any actual business as a whore, but something told her this man wouldn't stand for anything less than total capitulation. That was a compact she was unwilling to make. She would either have to find a way around it by picking men who were too drunk to know the difference and convincing them they'd had their bells rung, or she was only going to have one night or two at the most to discover a lead to the killer. She foresaw a confrontation with this man. Sizing him up she got the notion he possessed a brute strength that would be difficult for her to overcome. She mapped possible soft spots on his anatomy in case of emergency, but doubted even her fighting abilities would prove a match for him.

'What you looking at, you dumb whore?' The words shook her from her thoughts. She realized she had made a slight mistake. She'd taken too long to get his meter, made it too obvious.

'Why, jest your handsome self, sugar.'

He grabbed her arm, his fingers digging in. Uttering a startled whimper, she resisted the urge to jam her foot into his southern parts. Blowing her cover so soon would get her nowhere. 'You listen to me, woman. I don't go for none of that sweet talk your type uses. You think you can make a man dance 'cause of what's under your skirt but it won't work with me. I take eighty per cent right off the top and if you don't make enough for my taste I take more. You got that?'

She nodded, wincing as his fingers tightened. 'I reckon we understand each other.'

'Good. There'll be no problems, then, will there?' He shoved her towards a woman who was standing a few paces to her left, behind her. 'Catherine'll show you the ropes while I go fetch some supplies. You best be ready to sell that little ass of yours tonight.'

She nodded as he stared at her for an uncomfortable period of time before leaving the saloon.

After he'd left, a peculiar silence seemed to fill the barroom. The other girls glanced at her, then went back to whatever they were doing. Tootie turned to the young woman, Catherine. This was her. Damn, but she was beautiful and Tootie instantly decided that that was worse than the brutal treatment she'd just received from the bar-owner. The young woman's hazel eyes glimmered like soft glass, though pain was etched deep within them. Auburn hair done in large loops cascaded about a thin face that remained somehow delicate, despite the too-red lips and heavy make-up. Standing barely over five feet, she was a bit thinner than Tootie but her ample bosom was enough to melt most any man and was perfectly displayed above a purple bodice trimmed with white frill.

'You're Catherine . . .' The words slipped out before she could stop herself and she knew the stunned expression on her face must have made her look idiotic.

'Yes.' The woman's voice was softer than she would have ever expected from a whore. 'He's a bastard.'

'What?' Tootie forced her composure to return for the second time.

'Pruitt. He owns this saloon and he's a bastard. You'd best just leave now while he's gone and never look back.'

'I can't . . .'

The woman's eyebrow raised. 'Why not? There's saloons all over the West. You don't need this one. He'll beat you if you don't bring in enough money, you know that? Once you're here you're stuck. You don't perform to his expectations he'll make it so you're no good for anyone else. Go now.'

Tootie jutted her chin, steadied her voice. 'Reckon I've got his number. He best not try it with me.'

Catherine laughed with a tone that called Tootie a foolish little girl who would have to learn things the hard way. 'You're mistaken if you think that.'

'You don't look so bad off . . .' Tootie countered, trying to size up the woman. Funny thing was, she didn't get the impression of a whore. She read something else, a woman with something more who had somehow been chained to a role that didn't suit her.

'Honey, I'm more bad off than you could ever know.'

'Why do you work here, then, if he's so awful?'

Catherine looked down, a hint of darkness washing across her face. When she looked back up her eyes had hardened with resentment, though Tootie felt it wasn't meant for her personally. 'I work here because I have nothing else anymore.'

52

'You could leave, way you told me to.' Some inner dignity to this woman made Tootie want to like her, yet at the same time hate her for whatever relationship she had had in the past with Hannigan. The reaction was irrational, something she usually wasn't given to, but she couldn't deny it.

'No . . .' Catherine shook her head, a wan smile prying at her lips. 'No, I can't leave. There's nowhere to go. And maybe I can help here.'

'Help? How?'

The smile grew forced. 'Never mind, it's not important. Whether you're foolish enough to stay is up to you. Just watch your back and do what he tells you. Don't ever sass him, either. He'll never touch you in the way men do, but he'll think nothin' of breaking all your fingers or an arm.'

'Pleasant fella.'

'You don't know the half of it.' Catherine reached out, grasping Tootie's hand. 'Come, I'll show you the upstairs. Only one room you'll want to stay clear of.'

Tootie's brow crinkled as Catherine led her towards the stairs. 'Why's that?'

'We haven't been able to get the bloodstains out of the walls and floor . . .'

As Hannigan stepped from the sawbones's office he drew a great breath of warm air, thankful to be out of the place. The preservative stench seemed embedded in his nostrils. He knew he'd long be struggling to get the sight of those jars filled with body parts out of his memory.

Walking along the boardwalk, he headed for the hotel, where he reckoned on passing a few hours before going to the saloon to meet Catherine. He'd made it half-way there when a man stepped in front of him, blocking his passage.

Hannigan stopped and surveyed the stranger, who wore a charcoal suit with a black cutaway coat, dark trousers, and a black Stetson. A Peacemaker weighted the man's right hip and a Bowie rested in a sheath on his left. Of medium height, he was wiry of build with dark hair showing from beneath the hat and a thick mustache that turned up at either end. Young, probably no more than twenty-three or four, his blue eyes peered from in deep dark pits, their gaze cold, glittering, focused on Hannigan. A tin star glinted on his vest.

'You're Hannigan.' His voice was deep, rumbling, and it wasn't a question, more an accusation.

'One and only. I take it you're the local law?' Hannigan corralled the man's gaze.

'Marshal Severin.' Hannigan caught a hint of some accent, but couldn't place it. Foreign, though, he felt certain. 'I'm thinking you are here for trouble, yes?'

The accent came thicker this time, as if the man worked at covering it with varying success.

'I'm here for a killer. You consider that trouble take it up with the county marshal. I reckon he'll vouch for me.'

The marshal nodded, his expression remaining deadpan. 'I know of you, Mr Hannigan. I have read much in pulp novels of your career. I cannot say I approve.'

'I reckon I wasn't lookin' for your approval.'

The man smiled; it wasn't a pleasant expression, more like the grin a fox gave a hen house with an open gate. Hannigan took an immediate dislike to the lawman, though that wasn't a first for him. He had seen the type too often: local law who figured they controlled anything and everyone in their jurisdiction. More often than not they had their hands deep in the local businesses of ill repute, gambling, whoring, the like. Something told him he would get little co-operation from this man.

'You'll need it if you're thinking of staying in my town long.' The accent was nearly gone this time.

'Just here long enough to find me a killer, then I'll be out of your hair. I'll stay out of your way if you stay out of mine.'

'Who asked you here?'

'Don't see how that's your business.'

The marshal's eyes narrowed a hair. He didn't like the answer and that satisfied Hannigan just fine.

'Everything in this town is my business.'

Hannigan ignored the statement. 'How'd you know who I was, anyway?'

The marshal didn't miss a beat. 'Saw you ride in. I asked the hotel man who you were. Recognized the name from the books. They kept me company on my journey.'

'Journey?'

'From Poland. I wanted to see the Wild West. Decided I liked it. Justice is so much . . . more free here.'

'You also decided you don't like me.'

'You do not mince words, do you, Mr Hannigan?'

'Not one to beat around the bush.'

'Very well. No, I do not like you or your type. I learned much about you from the books, enough to know you have no business in this town.'

Hannigan remained unperturbed. 'That so? Let's call a spade a spade, Marshal. It ain't my type that annoys you, least not in the sense manhunting bothers many folks. It's just that you brook no threat to your authority. You figure this is your town and if there's any killers to be brought to justice you'll be the one who'll do it. Willin' to bet damn few in this town make a move without you knowing it or approving it. That about right?'

The man grinned, and his small eyes narrowed. 'Tread lightly, Mr Hannigan. Enjoy your stay, but make it brief.' With that he brushed by Hannigan, jostling his shoulder. Hannigan stood his ground, but irritation flooded his veins. He had hoped to work with the local law, though that was always dicey given his reputation and methods. This time that option was off the table. He'd been in town no more than two hours and already he'd managed to alienate two of its citizens. That had to be some sort of record, even for him.

As he was about to start towards his hotel room the hairs on the back of his neck tingled, his manhunter's sixth sense kicking in.

Watched. He felt as if someone were watching him. His gaze roved, settling on the newspaper office across the street. A man stood in a doorway, his face long, nose aquiline, chin sturdy. He had brown wavy hair and an ink-stained apron over his boiled shirt. Hannigan figured him for the newspaper owner. The man frowned, then disappeared into his office. Yet the feeling of being watched persisted for no reason he could see. He shook it off and walked towards the hotel. The town was getting more unfriendly by the second.

Bertrand Mitre moved back behind the corner of a building after seeing Hannigan enter the hotel. Now he knew where the bastard was holed up. He'd lost track of the woman, but reckoned she had to be close by, likely in the same hotel.

A thin smile painted his thick lips. Damn, it was almost too easy, wasn't it? That manhunter's rep was looking like a load of cowchips now. Sonofabitch didn't even know he was bein' dogged. For a moment there Mitre thought the

fella had gotten wind of him somehow; he'd seen the
manhunter tense, glance about, but by the time Hannigan
turned in this direction, Mitre'd moved out of sight. He'd
decided the bounty man hadn't spotted him after all, was
just being cautious out of habit. Mitre grinned. 'Time's
gettin' closer, Hannigan,' he muttered. 'And revenge is a
dish best served bloody.'

CHAPTER FOUR

The saloon was operating at full tilt by the time the sun had slipped behind the distant mountains and shadows haunted the streets. A Durham haze clouded the air and raised voices punctuated the room. Cowboys jammed the tables, their hands clamped about cards and whiskey glasses. Tootie spotted a couple of bargals she hadn't been introduced to earlier; they expressed little interest in her other than occasional jealous or spiteful glances, likely because her arrival meant fewer prospects for them. Little did they realize she posed no competition.

The majority leaned towards the homely side – except for Catherine, a fact that annoyed Tootie more and more, as her mind conjured up paranoid suppositions of Hannigan's past with the auburn-haired beauty. Her emotions posed a problem, because she noticed Pruitt looking her way a couple times when she'd wandered lost in thought. The expression in his eyes told her she'd best not let that happen often.

Catherine stood behind her, near the long polished bar that ran along the south wall. Through the crowd's staccato laughter and whoops, Tootie heard the young woman's voice rise with a plea, but she couldn't make out the words. Pruitt stood next to the girl, his eyes hard chips and face a shade redder than it had been a moment before.

Tootie angled closer, hoping to get within earshot. She kept the movement natural, smiling honey at various cowboys, dragging her fingers across their shoulders in a provocative motion. She picked men too involved in their games to bother much with a woman, though one made a grab for her caboose. She sidled away with a coy smile; she would have preferred clocking him with a whiskey-bottle.

Catherine's face had tightened, fear dancing in her eyes, pinching her features.

'Christ, I thought I told you to show her the ropes?' Pruitt said, and Tootie's belly plunged. They were discussing her; that meant her cover was at risk and she wasn't ready to let that happen quite yet. She braced herself to go on the offensive just the same, in case Pruitt decided to strike the other girl. No matter how much Tootie wanted to dislike Catherine, she'd discovered herself warming to the young woman after they'd spent the better part of an hour talking. Catherine had come in from Wolf's Bend to the north. She acknowledged the move was a mistake but an aborted relationship with a goldmine-owner had left her in dire straits. Crushed dreams, she had said, fool's gold, though she hadn't been specific about the details. The young woman mentioned it wasn't the first time her dreams had gone down a wrong trail. Genuine pain clouded her eyes with the admission.

Tootie wondered if it involved Hannigan in some way, but quickly passed it off as her own jealous suspicions.

'I did, Jack, honest, I did. I showed her everything.' Catherine's voice tremoloed, and even beneath the heavy coating of pancake her features bleached bone-white.

'Then why the hell ain't she brought in any money yet? She purdier than all the rest of the whores in this dump, includin' you.' A sadistic edge sharpened his voice. He enjoyed belittling her, that was plain. 'Hell, I caught her standin' around staring off into the yonder twice. I'm startin' to think she ain't never whored before.'

'That isn't my fault, Jack. I never met her before today.'

'Hell it ain't! I put her in your charge, so it's your fault, far as I'm concerned. She don't earn out, I'll be takin' it out on you an' her both. You hear me?'

Tootie kept any betraying expression off her face, but her belly knotted. She had slipped up but hoped it would pass. In most barrooms she would have gotten away with far more, had done so many times before, but not with a man like Jack Pruitt, who jumped on any excuse to mistreat his gals.

'Jack, please, she'll work out, you'll see.' Catherine tried to move back a step but he grabbed her wrist and jerked up her arm. Pain flashed across the young woman's face.

'The only reason I don't take my fist to your pretty little face is 'cause damaged whores make less money. But you keep in mind I can hurt you places where no one will notice.'

She tried to pry his fingers from her wrist but he held her fast and in that moment Tootie didn't know whether the man was totally in control of his anger. She inched forward, her heart filling her throat, one hand rising to her bosom, just above the derringer beneath her bodice.

Jim Hannigan stepped from the hotel and gazed at the darkened street. Night had come quickly, as if a blanket had been thrown over the land. With it came a sense of darkness apart from the hour, a living, secret thing slithering about the streets, shadowy, lurking, hungry. A few cowboys, oblivious to the feeling, headed for the saloon and late-working shopkeepers were just closing up, igniting a hanging lantern or two outside their shops.

A killer stalked these night-blackened streets, a brutal maniac who hid in shadows, leaving only the gruesome remains of his victims. This was no outlaw or run-of-the-mill bank-robber. This was something different. So far he'd only taken whores, but would that change? Would he strike at wives and daughters in their homes, or did he have a reason for his focus? Did the killer know Hannigan was in town, tracking him? Would he remain in the shadows, silent until the manhunter left? Had he moved on?

Hannigan found any answer to those questions elusive at this juncture. The doc had provided him a method of murder, a sketch of a brutal man's deeds, but little else. Hannigan had seen men go loco and kill. But this . . . this wasn't the same. It spoke of calculation, method, direction, though to a purpose known only to the killer. This man knew what he was doing, and why.

The manhunter moved off the boardwalk and headed across the street towards the saloon a couple blocks down. He saw no sign of the marshal. While he would have liked to question the local law about the murders, their earlier encounter made that problematic. Severin didn't want him here and wouldn't be forthright with any information. He reckoned he couldn't blame a lawman for resisting his help; after all, Hannigan was a killer in his own right, working beyond the law. He chased down men at the behest of those who had lost someone close to them, a wife, a daughter, a son. Men didn't hire Hannigan for justice; they hired him for vengeance. Few whom

Hannigan went after made it back for trial. That fact rode the nerves of most lawmen, though he listed a number of them as helpful acquaintances, amongst them a Pinkerton contact. In Hannigan's judgement, Severin wasn't averse to a manhunter's methods, he was averse to anyone getting in his way, challenging his authority or making him look less than all-powerful.

Hannigan's hazel eyes focused on the saloon, from where a burst of laughter pulled him from his thoughts. He noticed his palms were suddenly damp, knew it had nothing to do with the warm night. The closer he got to the saloon the faster his heart beat. Nerves. A feeling he wasn't used to, but the notion of seeing Catherine again . . .

He had never expected it. And finding her working a saloon was something he could not have imagined in his wildest notions.

By now Tootie would be in place, if he knew her at all. That only added to his trepidation. Things had suddenly become a hell of a lot more complicated than he'd bothered planning for when he'd received Catherine's letter and come a-runnin'.

Do you still have feelings for her?

The thought startled him and he quickly gave it up. That was an old bone he had no desire to chew.

'Christ . . .' he muttered, stepping on the boardwalk in front of the saloon. Durham smoke drifted out into the night, pungent in his nostrils. Shouts and clinking glasses greeted him as he pushed trough the batwings and stood surveying the room. A decent crowd, mostly cowboys, a few businessmen, all on their way to being sick with the morning's light. It was always the same wherever he went. Except for the killer running loose.

As he surveyed the painted women in the barroom he spotted Tootie, her back to him, and his belly cinched. He had expected it, but it was still like skinny-dipping in icewater.

His gaze stopped. She was angled away from him, but even after these years, he recognized Catherine. The auburn hair, the slim bosomy figure. A swirl of emotions took him but he had no time to dwell on them. He was in motion without hesitation, threading his way through the tables towards her and the man holding her wrist.

He didn't know the man, other than placing him as the saloon-owner by his appearance, but he knew the look on his face. He recognized it from the men he had tracked down before, the look of an animal on the foam. The man's temper was a hair's breadth from obliterating any restraint that kept him from injuring the woman in his grip.

He saw Tootie edging forward, but managed to cut her off and save her from ruining her cover. The bar-owner didn't notice because his back was to Hannigan, but Catherine saw him coming and her face washed with relief. The bar-owner must have been in enough possession of his composure to realize from her expression that someone was coming up behind him because his head whirled and viciousness flared in his eyes.

'You best go about your business, fella, 'fore you regret it.'

Hannigan stopped, eyes narrowing, adrenaline surging through his veins. 'You're all the same.'

'What the hell you talkin' about?' The bar-owner relaxed his grip and Catherine pulled free, massaging her wrist.

Hannigan's eyes held the bar-owner's. 'Seen it before.

You're damn good at beatin' on those who can't defend themselves. Women, weaker men.'

The bar-man laughed, a mocking sound that told Hannigan he'd made a slight error sizing up the man. The 'keep didn't just pick on those weaker; he was just plain mean. 'You must be a damn fool, fella. All you new ones are. You come in here figurin' you're the biggest cock in the hen-house. But it ain't like that, no siree. This here's my place and in it I'm the law.'

'Leave her be.' Hannigan's voice held steady, unintimidated. 'I won't tell you again.'

'Haw, haw,' said the bar-owner, no humor in his tone. His face grew redder, obviously unused to any backtalk. 'You jest don't think you can come in here and tell me how to run my business, do you? These are my whores. I'll treat 'em any goddamn way I please. Get the hell out of here 'fore the marshal has to send the funeral man to carry you out.'

'No.' The word came low, cold, brooked no argument. The bar-owner knew it and his hand went into motion without another thought. He wasn't about to let some stranger waltz in and order him around.

The bar-keep telegraphed the blow and Hannigan avoided it without much effort. His own fist swung up in a vicious uppercut that collided with the bar-owner's jaw, snapping his head up with the sound of two blocks slamming together. The punch would have taken down nine out of ten men, but the fellow didn't move. His head came down and a smile spread over his lips, even as blood dribbled from his mouth.

The saloon went quiet. Men stared, open-mouthed and unbelieving at the manhunter. As if by some unseen signal, they burst from their chairs, moving back to the fringes of the barroom, forming a loose circle.

Tootie pulled Catherine out of the way, then stood in front of her, one hand at her bosom, prepared to go for the derringer if Hannigan needed help.

Any surprise Hannigan might have felt vanished. He knew he was in for a fight, one he might not win. The bar-owner grabbed two handfuls of Hannigan's shirt and whirled him around. The manhunter's feet left the floor before he could set himself. He went through the air, slammed down on a table. The table legs buckled and he landed hard on his back. Breath burst from his lungs. His hat flew off his head, settling in the sawdust a few feet away.

Partly stunned by the impact, he pushed himself onto his side, shaking his head to clear the cobwebs. 'Aw, hell . . .' he muttered. He was getting too old for this, he reckoned, but he wouldn't get any older period if he didn't get to his feet and stop the bar-owner from pounding him into the sawdust.

The bar-owner lumbered towards Hannigan, one beefy hand grabbing for a Bowie at his waist.

Hannigan's legs wobbled as he reached his feet. His eyes focused on the bar-owner's, not the blade. He would see the move coming there a split second earlier and he needed every advantage now that the fight had taken on a deadly edge.

The 'keep swung the knife in a crisp arc, underhanded, nearly slicing a chasm across Hannigan's belly. The blade-tip streaked across the material of his shirt, but didn't go through.

Pruitt brought the knife back instantly, but Hannigan was ready for it. He sidestepped, catching the man's arm in an elbow lock. In the same motion he twisted, tried to snap the bone.

Pruitt was too strong. He hurled Hannigan around and sent him stumbling half across the barroom. Hannigan managed to get his balance before going over a table. The bar-owner hurtled forward, knife out-thrust.

Timing, his mind whispered. One misstep and the blade would plunge into his belly.

Pivoting, Hannigan snatched a whiskey bottle from a table standing to his right. In nearly the same motion he faded sideways, bringing up the bottle in a short arc. The bottle clunked off the bar-owner's jaw as he came in; the blade and hand holding it whisked by Hannigan's left side.

The bar-owner, off balance, stunned, kept going. The knife hit the wall, embedding itself.

Hannigan didn't give his opponent the chance to yank it free. He lunged, swinging the bottle at Pruitt's temple.

Pruitt caught the motion from the corner of his eye and whirled to get out of the way, letting go of the knife stuck in the wall.

His equilibrium lost from the first blow, he couldn't avoid the second. The bottle glanced from his face, and he staggered a step, but quickly recovered. He swung a sloppy punch that seemed to come from the floor. Hannigan, thrown off balance from the force of his swing, managed to avoid the brunt of it but Pruitt's fist thudded off his shoulder and propelled him sideways. Pain skewered his arm down to his fingertips. The bottle dropped from his grip and rolled across the floor.

With his heart pounding in his throat, sweat streaming down his face, Hannigan stopped his sideways lunge and set himself. Placing his weight on one leg, he pivoted, snapping the other leg up in a roundhouse kick that took

Pruitt square in the belly as he rushed in.

Air exploded from the bar-owner's lungs; he staggered. Hannigan seized the advantage, planted his feet and launched a three-punch combination. Each blow slammed into the man's jaw with a thunderous clack. The bar-owner blinked, teetered. Hannigan drove another uppercut into his chin.

The sound of the blow rang nearly as loud as a gunshot in the hushed silence of the barroom. Pruitt stumbled backwards, knees going in two different directions. He fell against the wall just below the embedded knife, panting, blood streaming from his nose and mouth.

Hannigan gasped, moved in to finish the fight before the man recovered.

Pruitt came half-up, grabbed the knife from the wall and yanked it free. He whirled, on his knees, arm cocked.

Hannigan's hand went for the Peacemaker at his hip. Although exhausted, his muscles trembling from exertion, the move was a fluid motion that suddenly saw the four-inch sawed-off barrel jammed against Pruitt's forehead.

'Give me a goddamned excuse,' Hannigan said through his teeth. ' 'Cause right now I got a notion to get even for every bargirl you must have hurt.'

Sweat ran down the bar-owner's face. His eyes narrowed, studying Hannigan intently, as he weighed his chances of putting a knife in the manhunter's belly before he could pull the trigger. The 'keep was a bully but apparently had no desire to check out of his earthly plain just yet.

Pruitt inched the knife downward and back into the sheath at his waist.

Hannigan kept the gun pressed to the man's forehead. 'I'm tellin' you this only once. I get wind you raised a hand to any of these girls in here and I'll come back and finish what we started. I won't even give you a warning, I'll just blow your brains clean out to the next town. We understand each other?'

Pruitt glared, hatred bleeding from his eyes, but nodded.

Hannigan moved back, holstering his gun, while watching the bar-owner climb to his feet. Pruitt dragged a forearm across his mouth, wiping away blood, keeping his eyes locked on the manhunter for a dragging moment. Then without a word, he went back behind the bar.

Hannigan turned, stopping as his gaze fell upon the marshal, who stood just inside the batwings. For a moment he wondered if the man were going to arrest him. Technically Hannigan was in the bar-owner's domain and if he wanted to press charges the marshal would have a right to hold him in a cell until matters got straightened out.

Severin glanced at the bar-owner, who shook his head. The marshal's gaze went back to Hannigan, a small smile drifting onto his lips. A few seconds later, he turned and left the saloon.

The crowd returned to their tables, hushed voices buzzing over the fight. A few glanced at him with a peculiar sort of reverence, while others appeared more concerned with getting back to their poker games.

Hannigan located his hat and the whiskey bottle he'd used on the bar-owner. He tossed the hat on to a table and lowered himself into a seat. He noticed Tootie pretending not to look at him, as she mingled with the patrons.

'It's been a long time, Hannigan,' Catherine said, as she came up to his table. 'You still know how to make an entrance, I see.'

Hearing her voice again did something to him, stirred things inside he'd thought long dead. He popped the top on the bottle and took a swig, the liquor's bitter flavor blending with the metallic taste of his own blood. 'Care to join me?' He set the bottle down.

She smiled a feeble smile, lowered herself into a chair after first glancing at the 'keep, who flashed her a look of fury, but made no move to stop her. 'He'll take it out on me later for this.'

Hannigan shook his head. 'No, he won't, not if he plans on livin' out the week.'

'It's good seein' you again, Jim.' Her gaze lowered, then she placed her hand over his. 'I missed you.'

An electric feeling sizzled through him at her touch, and he glanced over to see Tootie looking their way, an expression flashing across her face that revealed more than she probably wanted it to. He reckoned he'd be hearing about it later.

Drawing his hand away, he peered at the young woman, trying to recollect exactly how she had looked the last time he said goodbye to her. A few lines now that hadn't been there then, maybe, a fragile weariness, but she was still beautiful beneath the war paint. 'What the hell happened to you, Catherine?'

Something in his tone must have given away his guilt because she laughed. 'Don't worry, Hannigan, you didn't do this to me. I got over you.'

'Good to hear.' He wasn't sure whether to be relieved or injured.

Her hazel eyes clouded with pain. 'I met a fella after you – long after, maybe a year. He made a lot of money in the gold-mining industry. I married him. I didn't realize that everything he had was only a possession to him, just another golden trinket with which he could boast how powerful he was, how much he had. After a month he stopped touching me in a husbandly way. A month later he touched me in other ways, hitting me until I couldn't even stand up some nights.' She shook her head, frowned. 'He would tell his friends I had taken ill, or had fallen. They knew better, but didn't care. He took care of them too well. I took as much as I could, more than I should have. At last I got brave enough to leave, but I didn't count on just how much pull he had in that county. No one would hire me. I was desperate. I had one choice if I was going to survive . . .'

'This,' completed Hannigan. 'Don't rightly see how you traded up.' He glanced back at the bar-owner, who still kept his eyes on them.

'You don't understand. I was run out of town. I had no money, just the clothes on my back. You got no right to judge me.'

He heard a tremble in her voice, saw hurt in her eyes. And maybe even a peculiar sense of pride. 'I ain't judging you. But I won't sit here and say I approve, either.'

'I don't need your approval, Hannigan. Just your help.'

He might have called her a liar then; he heard the plea in her voice. If she didn't need his approval, she wanted his understanding.

'You could have found something else, Catherine. There's better things out there . . .'

'Are there? Where? Maybe you'll just ride in here and whisk me away from all this, way you gallantly fought for my honor against Pruitt?' Her eyes suddenly lifted, and he noticed Tootie's gaze shifting from them the moment Catherine caught her looking their way. The auburn-haired woman's focus returned to Hannigan.

He searched for words, finding them elusive. She was right, he had no right to judge her, no right to tell her how to live her life. But could he offer her anything more? He didn't like the conflict brewing inside him, the old feelings boiling up. So he relied on reflex, finding it easier to avoid confronting any leftover emotions he might have fostered for Catherine Tretlow.

His gaze lifted to a spot across the room, and his voice lowered. 'Your letter said three gals had been murdered . . .'

She laughed, the expression humorless. 'Same old Jim Hannigan, I see.' She waited for him to give her something, anything, but he couldn't oblige. She was right, he hadn't changed. Maybe he couldn't.

'I saw the doc. He gave me the how of the killings. Suppose you give me the why?'

She looked away, eyelids fluttering, hurt in her eyes again. When she gazed back at him a certain hardness had taken hold, one he reckoned she had mastered since becoming what she was now, a woman who sold herself for money.

'Three girls, like I said. One was killed in a room upstairs; that was Annie. Another died in a courtyard nearby, name of Polly. A third on a street near here; she was named Liz.'

'You knew them?'

'Not well. The girls in this place don't get friendly with each other much. Can't afford to with Jack' – she nudged her head towards the bar-owner – 'taking most of our money. Don't pay to encourage the competition.'

'Anyone see anything, hear anything?' He took a another swig of the whiskey, set the bottle down.

'Nothing. No one heard a thing, like the killer was

71

ghost or something.'

'Anyone have anything against the gals? They cheat anyone? Any husbands who might not want them talking?'

She shrugged. 'Not that I know of. Polly, she had a man sometimes, that half-breed at the edge of town.'

'Aaron Darkwolf.' He raised an eyebrow.

'That's the fella. How'd you know about him?'

'Doc mentioned him. Seems this Indian has a reputation.'

'Folks don't much like Indians around here but you if ask me you don't need look no further than behind the bar for the killer.'

'The bar-owner?'

'Jack Pruitt. He carries that knife with him everywhere. Threatens the girls with it, too, says he'll cut pieces off them if they don't make more money. Saw him hold it to a man's throat he had a disagreement with.'

Hannigan thought it over. He had two suspects, Pruitt and Darkwolf. He doubted having a parley with the barman was an option at this point. Still, the man was obviously violent, fast with a knife. Hannigan saw a possible third man to add to the list: Doc Francis. A man who collected body parts in jars and expressed a dislike for whores couldn't be written off, though it seemed a long shot.

'What reason would he have to kill them? They worked for him. Seems like he'd be hurting his source of income.'

She gave a slight shake of her head. 'You saw his temper.'

He nodded. 'Why do you care about these girls enough to call on me? Couldn't have been easy sending that note after the way we . . .' He stopped, knowing it was the wrong direction in which to lead the conversation.

She looked at the table, her finger tracing a bottle stain. Chewing on her lower lip, she looked back to him. 'It wasn't. It hurt when you left, Jim. I can't deny that. Took me some time to come to terms with it. Maybe I never did completely. But these gals, they're me. Least in some ways. They all deserved better than what happened to them, and they all deserve to rest in peace.'

He smiled. 'Same old Catherine, too.'

She uttered a gentle laugh. 'Folks change, but they don't.' Her face went serious again. 'This killer isn't going to stop unless someone stops him. No one else I know has a chance of doing that, except you.'

'He might just have moved on. Lots of drifters in these parts, assuming he isn't Pruitt or Darkwolf or some other local.'

'Doesn't matter. If he did, find him before he kills somewhere else. I read about you since you left. I know you charge a lot for your services and I don't have much money . . .'

He heard something coming, something behind her words that made his belly plunge.

'Don't, Catherine. I'll take this case as a favor to you, out of respect for what we had and maybe even a little guilt over it. But don't offer me something that has no meaning.'

Her features dropped and tears shimmered in her eyes. 'It might have meaning, Hannigan.' She placed her hand over his again and he wanted to pull away, but didn't move for a lost moment.

He stood then, drawing a deep breath and looking off towards the batwings. 'I'll see what I can find. In the meantime, don't walk the streets here at night and don't let the other girls go out alone.'

Her eyes widened. 'You're joking, right? How do you reckon I could stop whores from walking the streets at night?'

His face heated, and he knew it had been a foolish thing to say, but he was flustered by her touch and his mouth was working before his thoughts again. 'Do your best. Least give me some time to look into things.'

'You staying at the hotel?'

He didn't answer, hearing more behind the question than he was ready to deal with. Grabbing his hat, he started towards the batwings.

'Jim?' she said behind him, and he stopped, turning to see her standing beside the table.

'Yeah?'

'We had some good times, didn't we? I mean, before you left.'

He looked at the floor, then at her. 'Reckon we did at that.' He left the saloon before she could stir up any more conflict within him than she had already.

Tootie had watched the exchange with a sinking feeling in the pit of her stomach. The way they looked at each other, the way Catherine gently placed her hand over his – *twice*. They had been something, all right, maybe something special. Worse yet, embers of that fire still burned beneath the ashes.

Emotions clutched in her throat and tears shimmered in her eyes. Dammit, she never let herself indulge in such girlish things. She was as tough as any man and if Hannigan wanted some whore then let him have her! She'd only wasted a few months of her life. He'd never promised her anything anyway. Far from it.

No, that wasn't fair. Nothing in his actions indicated he

wanted that woman. It was just an old flame flickering. They never lasted. Did they?

'You won't reach that one . . .' The woman's voice came from beside her, jerking Tootie from her thoughts. She saw Catherine staring at her, likely wondering about the raw emotions splashed across her face. Catherine's own face appeared harder now, lips set in firm lines, the hint of competition reflected in her eyes.

'What?' She fumbled for words, finding none. She struggled to force her heart out of her throat.

'Jim Hannigan. I saw the way you looked at him. You tried to hide it but another woman knows.'

'Reckon I don't know what you're talkin' about. He's just another good-looking fella, that's all.'

Catherine offered a thin smile. 'Is it? You know him from somewhere?'

Tootie shook her head, maybe a bit too fast. 'I don't know him at all . . .' Her tone darkened, a note of spite riding it that she couldn't suppress.

Catherine studied at her, searching her eyes, but Tootie had recovered enough to hide anything she didn't want seen. A defense mechanism, one she was damn good at and one a few moments of weakness couldn't take away.

Catherine nodded and her gaze flicked to the batwings. 'Like I said, you'll never reach that one. Stay clear.' The woman was staking her claim where Tootie figured she had no right. She couldn't argue it without giving away her association with Hannigan, but it didn't stop her from asserting her own territory.

'Why, honeybun, nice lookin' fella like that's fair game. I reckon he'll get lonely one of these nights.'

Catherine laughed, an expression that called Tootie a fool. 'No, he won't. Least not lonely enough to let a whore into his bed . . .' She walked away, leaving Tootie staring at the batwings and praying the last part of what the woman had said was true.

Tootie scanned the darkened street as she made her way along the boardwalk towards the hotel. She picked out every nook where a man might hide, scoured every shadow. At this late hour, with a killer running loose, she wasn't about to let her guard down the way she had earlier in the saloon. She paused, a chill trickling along her spine. A feeling, vague yet unsettling, washed over her. She felt unseen eyes focused on her, but saw no one. Even most of the noise from the saloon had died down. A breeze stirred dust in the street, made hushed sounds slithering around buildings. A sign creaked.

'You're letting your nerves get to you,' she told herself, starting forward again, doubling her vigilance.

When she reached the hotel, she let her body go rubbery, began to stagger. She would need to get past the clerk again and it would easier if she pretended to be in a condition unconducive to questioning.

She hurled open the door and half-tumbled across the threshold, then weaved as she headed for the stairway. The scrawny clerk looked up, puzzlement on his face.

'You back?' He studied her face and she wondered if he weren't thinking about her resemblance to Hannah Garret.

Half-turning away from him, she wavered, looking as if she would fall on her face with the slightest gust. 'Whys I got a man waitin' on me, sugar. Wouldn't do to keep him a-waitin', now, would it? Big spender, this gent is.' She made her words slushy and slid her first two fingers against her thumb.

'You're new in town, ain't you? Reckon I know all the whores.'

'Just came in t'other day, honeybun. Reckon you must have missed the incoming stage.'

His brow crinkled and for a moment she doubted he believed her. 'I usually get a cut from ones I set the clientele up with. Free agents ain't welcome.'

Tootie reached into her skirt and drew out a two-dollar bill, then staggered over to the counter and tossed it before the man. She reckoned that would solve his nosiness for the time being, at least. 'How's 'bout you and me make us-selves a bargain, sugar. I slip you a percentage and you let me come an' go any way I please.'

'Why should I do that?' But his eyes were fixed to the Hamilton.

'Why, because I'm the by-damnedest purdiest whore you ever got in this here town, I reckon. I'll bring you in more than all the other gals put together.'

He nodded, the notion sitting well with him. 'Reckon I see your point. Just don't make no trouble.'

'Little ol' me?' She giggled. 'Why, trouble's the furthest thing from my mind. I'm just a plain ol' working gal.'

He uttered a chopped laugh and she smiled, then headed for the stairway again. She felt his gaze on her back but the promise of future payments kept him from acting on any suspicions he might have entertained.

After reaching the top of the stairs, her manner changed. After making sure no one was about, her carriage straightened and her walk grew confident, purposeful. She went to Hannigan's room, drew a breath, then tapped on the door.

Hannigan sat on the edge of the bed, his face in his hands.

77

Seeing Catherine again had proved more difficult than he thought it would. He wondered just how much he still felt for her, how much was the rosy gloss time sometimes paints on the past. Had he made a mistake in leaving her? Had there been more to their relationship than he allowed himself to consider at the time?

One thing was certain, her touch had sent a ripple of desire through him that he would never have admitted to Tootie.

Dammit, this just complicated things that didn't need complicating. He should have been over any past feelings for her and honestly thought he had been when he decided to come at the request of her letter. Wasn't the tornado of emotions he had to deal with each day around Tootie enough? Did he need to go adding to it? He should have known better and this whole thing had the potential to blow up in his face.

But what could he do? While they hadn't parted on the best of terms, he clearly recollected telling her the day he left if she ever found herself in some kind of trouble he would come if she needed him. Maybe he hadn't really figured on her taking him up on it, because it was just one of those promises someone made when they didn't know how the hell else to desert a crying woman.

You're a bastard.

No denying that. But he was also a man who kept his word.

What she had become . . . it made no sense to him. She'd left one abusive situation for another. Maybe it was something he had missed in her when they were together, some flaw he had overlooked and set free the day he left.

There you go being arrogant again, Hannigan. The world don't revolve around you, or haven't you heard?

Yet if there were even a slim chance that he owned some small part in her fate, he owed her something now, a chance to break away from her life.

What if she don't want that?

She did, he saw it in her eyes. Had he offered she still would have ridden away with him, as if no years had passed.

'That what you want?' he asked himself, voice a whisper against his palms.

A tapping at the door left the query unanswered. His head lifted from his hands and he stared at the door a moment, before getting up to go to it. One hand on the handle, the other on his Peacemaker, he opened the door to see Tootie standing outside, forearm braced against the sill, a coy look on her face.

'Lookin' for a good time, sugar?'

He frowned. 'Get in here 'fore that nosy clerk comes on up.'

She laughed. 'Oh, I think I got his number, least for a spell.'

He gave her a puzzled look but she didn't elaborate. He closed the door, went to the window and, folding his arms, leaned a shoulder against the wall. 'Find out anything?'

She shook her head. 'More than I wanted, but nothing to do with the case.' Her tone had sobered and for once his better judgement told him not to ask what she meant by the statement.

'Nothing?'

She shrugged. 'Tried talking to a couple of the other girls after you left, but they didn't know much of anything. Three girls, all killed brutally, one of 'em right upstairs in the saloon. The girls don't talk much with each other, so personal comings and goings aren't noted. A few allusions to the bar-owner being at the heart of it, or maybe an Indian living near the edge of town.'

'Aaron Darkwolf. He spent time with one of the murdered girls, Polly. I plan on looking into him right soon. The bar-owner . . . he's certainly the type to brutal-ize women or stick a knife in anyone who gives him trou-ble. Doctor I talked to was a mite peculiar, too, and does-n't have any love for whores. But I gotta ask myself why would any one of them suddenly start butchering women? The bar-owner makes money off them. He might beat one of them to death, maybe even cut her throat without much provocation, but these murders, they go way beyond that.'

'Still, temper management isn't his strong suit. Maybe he couldn't stop himself.' Tootie folded her arms. Lanternlight twinkled from her mahogany eyes, glowed softly on her skin.

'Reckon . . . then there's Darkwolf. Maybe he'd kill his girlfriend, but why the other two?'

'Unless there's some connection we haven't discovered yet.'

He nodded. 'And the doctor, got the notion he's ridin' a bit crooked in the saddle, but from the weathered look of his sign he's been in town a spell. Why suddenly start killing now?'

'Maybe he just went loco.'

'Maybe, but whoever's responsible for these murders is sane enough to avoid getting caught. He's got a reason for picking these women, an agenda. And crazy or no, a man who would do something like this . . .'

'Won't stop.' She frowned. 'Whores make perfect targets. Easy to isolate, law won't bother looking into it much.'

'Marshal made it plain he doesn't want my help.'

Tootie looked at the floor, her expression darkening. 'Who is she, Jim? Please, be honest with me this once.'

He drew a deep breath, his stomach cinching. Looking out the window, he hoped none of his thoughts from a few moments before showed on his face.

He looked back to her. 'She . . . she's someone I knew a lifetime ago.'

'I figured as much. Now tell me who she was to you?' Her gaze locked with his.

'We met while I was on a case. I was tracking down a man who robbed a stage and killed a woman who worked at a dress-shop with Catherine. Catherine came from a good family, but they died when she was barely fourteen. Her aunt raised her, but they weren't close. She and I talked some about the murdered girl, and some of what she told me led to the killer. Turned out the man was the girl's fiancé. The stage robbery was a ruse to cover the fact the girl had found out he was wanted for another robbery and was going to tell the law.'

'But you didn't leave after the case was finished?' He heard a hint of accusation in her voice.

'No, I didn't. I saw her a few more times, but I realized she was getting close—'

'And so were you.' She said it as fact, not letting him shift any blame to the woman.

He nodded after a moment. 'Reckon I was.'

She gave him an odd expression he couldn't read. 'Let me guess the rest. You got scared and ran off . . .'

The way you were gonna run off on me . . . She didn't say it, but he heard the words plain as could be in the way her voice trailed off. She suddenly looked harder, more unsure that he really wouldn't have left had she not shown up at the stable that day in Revelation Pass.

'Tootie . . .'

'I get it, Jim. She fell in love with you and you were falling for her. Or maybe you had already fallen. Whatever the case, there's unfinished business between the two of you. I saw it tonight in the way she looked at you, the way she touched you.'

He waited, tensing for her next words, ones that would accuse him of reciprocating those feelings. But they didn't come.

'It wasn't like that.' Was he lying? Likely. Maybe he had loved Catherine; maybe he had just done what he always did whenever he got close and old nightmares told him a settled life wasn't for him.

'Wasn't it?' Her lips quivered and her eyes looked glassy with tears. 'Did you take her to your bed? Promise her anything?'

He glanced back out the window, swallowing hard. 'I don't think so.'

'What the hell do you mean "you don't think so"? You lie with her or not?'

'No . . . I did not.' He turned back to her. 'But I don't think I promised her anything, either. I told her I wasn't ready to settle down, didn't know if I ever would be. I told her I had to leave.'

'Will you tell me that, too?'

'Tootie—'

'Christ, Jim, what do you expect me to think? You play with folks' feelin's and just expect them to go on like nothing ever happened?'

'You're being irrational.' Damn, that wasn't what he wanted to say.

'You haven't seen irrational yet. I'm just getting started. I got the notion from you we had something. I thought it was special, a one-time thing and you were just having a hard time dealin' with letting me get close to you for some reason I didn't know. Now I find out you got a history of it. And now I gotta wonder, am I gonna wake up and find you gone? Or am I gonna lose whatever the hell it is we have to someone else?'

'I never made you any promises.' Christ, he was still getting the wrong words out and growing more agitated by the second, mostly because she was hitting him right where he was vulnerable. He had no defense for his behavior, and he couldn't offer her the assurances she wanted or, at the moment, would believe.

'No, you didn't. Just the way you didn't make her any.' Tootie whirled, grabbed the handle and yanked open the door. Pausing, she looked back to him. 'You know what? I won't wait around forever, Mr Hannigan. You best decide whether there's a promise you want to make to someone for once in your life. And you best decide whether whatever secrets that keep you from being more than a cold machine are worth the price you gotta pay.'

'We all got secrets, Tootie . . .'

'Reckon we do. I'm willin' to share mine. You say the same?' He looked at the floor, struggling to keep his emotions in check. 'I didn't think so . . .' he heard her whisper, then the door shut. After she'd left a hollowness washed over him like nothing he'd ever felt.

'You're a bastard all right,' he whispered.

Tootie leaned against the window sill, staring out into the night. A tear slid down her cheek, smearing the coral. Had she pushed too hard? Did she have the right to? His past belonged to him, after all, the way hers did to her. But his came with something unfinished. Hers did not. She'd vanquished her ghosts; his had come back to haunt them both.

Catherine Tretlow was a beautiful woman and she and Hannigan had a connection, a past bond. Tootie had only known him a few months and while they had been through a lot together was it enough to overcome a lost love?

He left that woman, she reminded herself. And if what you got with him is strong enough you'll get past this and he won't leave you.

He had almost left her, another voice countered. Would he have ridden away had she not caught him? she asked herself again. That question lingered between them, despite his denials, and it was one she couldn't live without an answer to. She wouldn't spend whatever time they had left wondering whether she'd wake up to find him gone. He owed her at least that much.

Movement on the street below caught her eye, drawing her from her thoughts. A saloon girl, the one named Mary Ryan if she recollected right, who'd told her about the Indian, was staggering along the boardwalk.

'Damn fool . . .' Tootie muttered. She lifted the window, which was open only a couple inches, and leaned out.

'Hey, get the hell off the street. You lookin' to get done like those other girls?'

The woman paused, looked up at her, letting out a sharp laugh. 'Don't you worry none, missy. I can take care of myself. That sonofabitch won't get me.' She laughed again then stumbled along, disappearing into the shadows.

Tootie shook her head. 'Lord protect the foolish . . .' She lowered the window and went to the bed, praying she'd be able to sleep but knowing she'd be up most of the night dwelling on what she'd seen between Catherine and Hannigan in the saloon.

CHAPTER FIVE

Shouts and excited chattering reached Jim Hannigan's ears as he stepped from the hotel with the sunrise. Sleep had proved elusive, the argument with Tootie weighing on his mind the entire night. His limbs felt heavy with fatigue and his mind cloudy from the lack of shut-eye. Good thing he'd figured on an early start, because he doubted he could have stayed in bed staring at the ceiling a moment more.

He had put Polly's Indian boyfriend first on his list, but the situation in the street changed things. He could tell from the shocked looks and nervous voices that something terrible had occurred. Women's faces looked pale in the amber sunlight and angry curses spat from a number of the men.

Hannigan stopped a man, a frail-looking fellow wearing an apron who looked to be a storekeeper.

'What's the ruckus about?' he asked.

The man peered at him, eyes wide. ''Nother whore got herself cut to pieces. Fourth one, fella.'

'What?' Hannigan's brow furrowed.

'Next street over, in a small courtyard. Phillips from the gunshop always comes to work with the roosters. He stumbled on her and let out a god-awful scream. Heard it all the way from the end of town, I did, and came a-runnin'. Ain't never seen the likes of what happened to that girl. Won't be forgitting 'bout it till my dying day.'

Hannigan nodded. 'Thanks . . .' He stepped past the man and headed against the tide of townsfolk towards the street the man had indicated. He spotted a black-suited form ahead, his back to the manhunter. He paused, watching the man. The marshal just stared at a spot in a small wrought-iron-railed courtyard.

'What the hell you want here, Mr Hannigan?' the marshal asked without turning. Hannigan wondered what had given him away.

The marshal turned to him, his face dark, strained, with something in his eyes that Hannigan couldn't read. 'I saw your shadow, if that's what you're wondering. It's the little things that give you away . . .'

'Could have been anyone's shadow.' He stepped closer to the marshal, passing through a gate into the courtyard. The fact the man had known it was him irritated him for no particular reason.

'Everyone else is walking away from this spot. Only one who'd be walking towards it is someone interested in knowing what happened. I figured that to be you, yes?' The man's accent came stronger than it had a moment before.

'What happened?' Hannigan ignored the man's superior attitude.

'Thought I made it clear I didn't want your help?'

'Thought I made it clear it wasn't a matter of choice. You want me to get an order from the territorial marshal and make it official?' He held the man's gaze. The marshal remained silent a moment, then began twisting at the end of his mustache.

'Mary Ryan. Whore. Butchered same as the rest. That's about all there is to tell.'

'Suppose you fill in the details for me, including the three others.'

The marshal walked away from him, to a dark area on the ground. The signs of the savagery of the attack were obvious. Crimson had soaked into the dirt in an uneven pool. He couldn't recollect ever seeing so much spilled blood.

'Happened right here. But I am thinking you know that.' The man's accent grew thick for a moment, then mellowed. 'The others you likely already know all there is to know about, since I heard you were asking a whore at the saloon.' He turned back to Hannigan, daring him to deny the fact.

Hannigan guessed the marshal had found someone at the saloon who had overheard him, or had made an accurate guess based on the events at the barroom last night. The manhunter nodded. 'I got the overview. I'm looking for some small detail a whore might leave out.'

The marshal's chin lifted a fraction. 'Likely she told you all there was. Polly Maybrick, Annie O'Dell, Elizabeth McBride. All of them butchered the same way as Mary Ryan. No sign of the murderer, left no clues in the room or on the street.'

'What about the bar-owner or Polly's boyfriend, Darkwolf?'

The marshal raised an eyebrow. 'What about them?'

'Either strike you as a killer?'

'Both. But they didn't do this.'

'You got a hook to hang that hat on?'

'For what reason should they kill their livelihood? Makes no sense.'

'Reckon I see where the bar-owner would lose money but Darkwolf?'

The marshal uttered a short laugh. 'Well known he lived off her. He doesn't make enough with those skins he sells and he's a drunk . . .'

'I sense a "but" behind that.' Hannigan held the man's gaze. For a moment the marshal didn't move, then with a wave of his hand he gestured at Hannigan to follow him. The lawdog led him to the back wall of a building that flanked the courtyard.

Hannigan's gaze froze on the wall. In chalked scrawl, the words arcing and uneven, some letters large, some small, was written:

The Engins are The men that Will not be Blamed for nothing.

'Engins . . . Injuns . . .' Hannigan muttered, his brow furrowing.

'Indians.' The marshal nodded.

'The townsfolk notice this?'

'A few of them, I think so.'

From his expression, the marshal was thinking the same thing that had occurred to Hannigan. Something like this was just the fodder to incite a vigilante mob. Maybe with the killings limited to whores that wouldn't happen immediately, but it was the kind of seed that wouldn't take much fertilizing to make it spring to life.

'Where's the body?'

'Sent it to Francis.'

'Why? You don't seem too concerned about whores, considering what happened to the bodies after he finished with them.'

The marshal's face reddened a bit but he kept his composure. 'Whores are a blight on a controlled society, Mr Hannigan. Someday the world will be rid of them completely. There will be fewer crimes, security for decent folk. It is the first step towards Utopia.'

'You sound a lot like the doc, Severin.'

The marshal nodded. 'We are of like minds, I believe. He sees the plight that society faces, knows what ensures its survival. Besides, someone has to witness the killings.'

'Reckon I don't catch your meanin'.'

'They were whores. No relatives, that I'm aware of. No one to see what became of them. Just disposable women.'

Hannigan studied the man but couldn't fathom his meaning. Maybe something was lost in the translation from his native language to English, but one thing was certain: he saw not even a hint of compassion for the dead women in Severin's eyes.

Hannigan ducked his chin at the wall. 'These words seem to blame Darkwolf, yet you don't think he did the killing.'

The marshal shrugged. 'Anyone could have written them. Someone might be trying to blame the Indian, but maybe I change my mind about him if I think it over long enough.'

'Even assuming he killed Polly, why kill the other girls?'

The marshal shook his head. 'Who knows what Indians will do?'

'Take it you share the doc's opinion there, too?'

'I care not one way nor the other.'

Hannigan's gaze settled back on the writing. 'You got a photographer here in town?'

'Yes. But this message will be gone by the time you get him here.' Severin's accent faded again, taking on a western twang. 'Enough folks saw it already. I won't tolerate mob justice. That Indian's guilty, I will bring him in myself.'

Hannigan reckoned it was pointless to argue with the man, but his desire to talk to Aaron Darkwolf ratcheted up a notch. On the face of it, the message looked like an obvious attempt to place blame. If the Indian had written it himself he was either monumentally stupid in chancing a mob coming after him, or as arrogant a sonofabitch as any man Hannigan had ever encountered.

Hannigan turned and walked to the spot where the girl had been killed. Kneeling, he studied the ground. He noted tracks in the dust, partials anyway, but too many feet had trampled through here since the discovery of the body to provide any lead. The blood pooled in one area; no trickles led away from the scene. He scrutinized the surroundings but quickly discovered that the trail was as dead as the young woman whose blood soaked the ground.

After another few moments, he gave up the investigation and started towards the street.

'Mr Hannigan . . .' the marshal said behind him.

Hannigan stopped, not bothering to look back. 'Yeah?'

'Consider my advice to you. You are not wanted here. They were only whores.'

'You so sure it won't spread beyond them, Marshal? Way I see it, a killer's a killer and those women, no matter what they were, deserve better. I aim to find this man. You have a notion to get in my way you best think it over careful.'

'Mr Hannigan, I think you mistake yourself for someone with authority in this town. You have none. Your threats mean nothing. Perhaps you should think things over careful yourself . . .'

The marshal was right. At this point he had no authority here, though a day's ride to the territorial marshal would fetch him some. His aversion to the man strengthened, made anger crawl through his veins like fire-ants, and he was tempted to argue it, but for now his better judgement won out. He drew a deep breath and walked away, leaving the marshal staring after him.

The first thing Hannigan noticed as he walked into the examination room at the doctor's office, besides the stench, was the body lying on the examination table, covered with a sheet. A gory patch of blood had soaked through the sheet and Hannigan knew this time the odor in the room came from the corpse. He'd smelled decaying bodies before; it was something a man never forgot, nor got used to.

Francis stood by the microscope. As Hannigan paused in the doorway, the doctor looked over to him. 'What are you doing back here?'

'Marshal told me he sent you the body.'

The doctor nodded. 'Just finished with it.' He walked over to the covered form and pulled back the sheet.

Hannigan had seen some gruesome sights in his day but he was ill prepared for the one that met him now.

'Jesus . . .' he muttered, wanting to look away, though riveted by a gruesome fascination to the form. The sight of that gutted body would haunt his nightmares until his dying day. If he hadn't known the body belonged to a woman . . .

Blood covered nearly her entire form. Her features were unrecognizable, carved-back flesh and crimson obliterating her face. Gaping holes shown in her chest and abdomen.

Unable to take the sight any longer, he motioned and the doctor drew the sheet back over the body. For one of the few times in his life, Hannigan struggled to find his composure. He couldn't get the gruesome image out of his mind.

'This what happened to the rest?' he asked at last, voice low.

The doctor smiled, a perverse humor in his eyes. 'Worse. Throat cut seven inches across, commencing below her left ear. Nearly severed her head and her right ear is missing. The abdomen was laid open from breast-bone to pubes, the flaps on either side drawn back. Killer placed her intestines beside her body.'

'I get the picture.' Hannigan moved deeper into the room, nauseated by the odor, heat flushing his face. Many would have called Jim Hannigan a hard man, one jaded by experience. They would have been only partly right. He'd never gotten used to the death of an innocent person, especially a death inflicted in such a horrible manner.

Francis raised an eyebrow. 'Really? There's more. I could give you the particulars. Fascinating, really.'

'That's a person on that table, Francis, not some speci-men.'

A placid smile filtered across his lips. 'Not any longer . . .'

'Suppose you just tell me what didn't match the rest.'

The doctor shrugged. 'Suit yourself. Her organs, ones she's got left at any rate, show signs of deterioration asso-ciated with alcoholism. Killer likely had more time with her, because the wounds were more brutal, as if whoever did it went into some sort of blood frenzy.'

'What do you mean by the ones she had left?'

'Killer took one of her kidneys.'

'Sure you don't have it in one of your jars?' More than a little disgust filtered into Hannigan's tone.

Francis showed a measure of annoyance. 'I'll hold onto the one left behind, for study, but, no, I had nothing to do with the one that's missing.'

'You reckon every run-of-the-mill outlaw killer would know where a kidney was located, then be able to extract it in a dark courtyard?'

'What are you implying, Mr Hannigan? I don't think I like what I'm hearing in your tone.'

'I'm implying nothing. Just asking if whoever took that kidney might have had some medical knowledge. Seems almost like he'd have to.'

'You're mistaken. Anyone familiar with basic anatomy could have done it, given enough time. Or perhaps a butcher, or animal skinner . . .'

Hannigan smiled an uneasy smile, folded his arms. 'Meanin' another trail right back to that Indian?'

'I prefer that explanation to the one you were insinuating. Am I to assume I am suspect because of my specimens and missing body-parts?'

'Whole damn town's suspect at this point, far as I'm concerned. This . . .' He ducked his chin at the body. '. . . means the killer's still here and ain't about to stop. I've got few facts to go on and they point to someone who hates whores and might have some knowledge of internal workings. That means you and that Indian go to the top of the list.' He didn't add that the words scribbled on the wall might also indicate someone who was looking to cast the blame on another, perhaps one who hated Indians as well as whores. But the scrawled writing and misspelling seemed on the face of it to indicate someone with less schooling than the doctor, though that might be an intentional misdirection.

'Maybe you should question Darkwolf, then. It might be enlightening.' A hidden meaning lurked behind the words, one Hannigan wasn't quite sure about.

Setting it aside for the moment, Hannigan asked, 'Where can I find this fella?'

'He lives in a shack at the edge of town. You can't miss it. Follow the stench.'

'Stench?'

'You'll know what I mean when you encounter it.'

Hannigan almost said it couldn't be any worse than the one in this room, but let it drop. 'This woman, the marshal told me her name was Mary Ryan.'

Francis nodded. 'Another useless life. But maybe a productive death, if I can learn something from her internals.'

'You're not exactly exonerating yourself, Francis. Talk like that makes me edgy.'

'Does it? Well, men like yourself seldom understand the need to advance science. Someday many lives will be saved because a few useless women contributed to the cause.'

Hannigan let out a disgusted sound. 'I reckon you asked her, she'd rather have her life back.'

'Well, asking her is beyond question, isn't it?'

Hannigan ignored the man's sarcasm. 'How long you been a sawbones here?'

'Five years next month. Why?'

'Jack Pruitt at the saloon, how long's he been here?'

The doctor shrugged. 'Don't know. He was here when I arrived. Far as I know he was born here.'

'Darkwolf?'

'Two years, maybe three. I really don't see what that has to do with anything.'

'Maybe nothing.' But the length of time put all three men relatively in the same position. Why would men with a history in this town suddenly start killing? 'Jack Pruitt, he got any medical knowledge you know of?'

'Pruitt's a violent man. I treated some of the men he . . . had differences with. Don't reckon he stopped to think about which organs he was bruising. Far as I can tell he just pounds away till they can't stand on their own anymore.'

'You ever treat any of his girls?'

'I don't treat whores.'

'See to it Mary Ryan gets buried proper.'

'What?' Genuine shock flashed across the doctor's face. 'Whatever for?'

'She deserves better than what became of those other women. Get the funeral man over here.' Hannigan fished a roll of greenbacks from his pocket, peeled off a number and tossed them on to a small table. 'That don't pay for it, tell him I'm easy enough to find at the hotel. I hear you did anything different, I won't be in a peaceable frame of mind the next time I come here.'

'You won't get on Tucker's good side that way. He was hopin' to fatten up those hogs a bit more.' A perverse glint came to the man's eyes with the jest and Hannigan decided that, as with the marshal, his aversion for this man had gone up a few notches.

'Not my job to get on anyone's good side. My job is to find this butcher and if I can give even one of them poor women a chance at peace, I'm obliged to do so.'

The doctor shook his head. 'Just whores, Mr Hannigan. Just whores.'

Hannigan's lips drew into a hard line. 'Just see to it you do what I said. Good Lord might forgive you for your judgements but I won't.' He turned and left the examination room, wondering just how much hatred the doctor had for the women and how far he would take it.

One thing the sawbones had hit dead on: Hannigan could have located the Indian's shack by the smell alone. The dwelling looked out of place compared to the rest of the buildings, and likely most folk in Miller's Pass wanted to forget it existed. Loose boards hung in abundance, and windows, paneless, were covered with thin tanned hide or nothing at all. The area to either side was overgrown, littered with animal bones, sections of crates and discarded pieces of rotting meat. The horrid stench surrounded the place like a foul cloud, the odor of decay and death. Closing his nostrils against it, he tried breathing through his mouth but soon discovered he could taste the awful reek, which was worse.

Alert for any signs of threat, he scouted the sides and back of the building, finding no one about. Darkwolf was no more than someone of interest in the case for the moment, but the Indian likely knew the attitudes of some of the townsfolk towards him and it wouldn't be much of a leap to figure on someone questioning him sooner or later. He might well be hostile and Hannigan wasn't about to take any chances with his staging an ambush.

Returning to the front, he rapped on the heavy door, waited. No response. Was the man out tracking?

'Darkwolf, you in there?' he shouted, banging a fist against the door this time. 'Name's Hannigan. I just want to talk to you.'

No sound came from within. Hannigan slid his hand around the brass handle and twisted, finding it unlocked. He pushed the door open. The reek that cascaded from within was ten times worse than anything outside. 'Jesus . . .' he muttered, stepping just inside the door. He paused, peering about the shabby room. The source of odor became instantly apparent. Animal skins hung from everywhere in the large room that served as living quarters, kitchen and parlor. They were tacked to walls, suspended from pegs above windows, draped over a small table and the back of a chair, stacked in corners. Most appeared recently skinned, and many smaller animals such as beaver and polecat gave off musky odors along with a metallic decay stench. He also noted deer, bobcat, even bear hides. One thing was obvious: Darkwolf liked killing things.

The reek and moist heat in the room set Hannigan's nerves on edge. The hairs on the back of his neck stood up in a tingling wave. Nothing outwardly pinpointed the man as a whore killer, but he couldn't quell an unsettled feeling brewing in his gut. Darkwolf would have some anatomical knowledge as far as animals were concerned; would he have it for humans as well? And would a man used to butchering have any compunction about murder? Normally the step from beast to man would have been too big for Hannigan to give serious consideration, but add it to the man's parasitic relationship with his dead girlfriend and the words scrawled on the courtyard wall and he couldn't rule it out, either.

A sound stopped his thoughts. For a moment he couldn't figure out what it was or where it had come from. Then he had it: it was the sound of a sharply inhaled breath . . .

Hannigan tried to throw himself forward, but was too late. A body came hurling at him from the rafters above his head. The Indian had braced himself between the beams, just over the door, a knife clenched in his teeth.

Darkwolf hit him with the force of a bull charging and Hannigan hurtled forward and down. He slammed into the puncheon floor on a shoulder and rolled instinctively, but pain splintered through his arm all the way to his fingertips. Stunned, he tried to push himself to hands and knees.

Somehow Darkwolf managed to land on his feet. He had the knife out of his mouth and in his right hand, and was nervously slashing it in a short arc back and forth before him.

'I know who you are, you sonofabitch.' His dark face was reddened with anger, his brown eyes hard, bloodshot. 'Heard your name before. Only one reason you would be here. Who told you I was responsible for killing Polly? That no-good sawbones? That sonofabitch marshal? Pruitt?'

Hannigan shook the cobwebs from his head, tried to get to his feet. Darkwolf lunged.

'I just came here to talk—' Hannigan started, holding up a hand as he got to his feet.

'Hell you did. You ain't blamin' me for those killin's. This town ain't blamin' me!' He thrust the blade at Hannigan's belly; the manhunter barely got out of the way. The half-breed couldn't have been much more than twenty-two or three, black hair long, unkempt, tangled about his face. He looked unwashed, specks of dried blood smeared on his face, blue shirt and buckskin trousers.

Darkwolf flashed a vicious expression, swept the blade in a backhanded arc. The tip sliced across Hannigan's shirt, skimming the material.

'Christ, will you just listen—'

The Indian laughed, a mocking, sharp tone. 'Why? So

you can help them stretch my neck? That's what they want in this town. Oh, maybe it ain't occurred to them yet to blame me, but it will.' Gritting his teeth, Darkwolf jabbed the knife towards Hannigan's heart.

Guilty or not, the Indian intended to kill him and would if Hannigan didn't give up trying to talk sense into him. The manhunter timed the thrust, sidestepped, snapped up an arm and locked the Indian's arm in the crook of an elbow, the same move he had used on Jack Pruitt with no success. This time, however, it worked. Darkwolf was powerful, but nowhere near as strong as Pruitt. He was also young, inexperienced, hadn't expected the move. He uttered a sharp grunt of pain as the manhunter twisted. The knife dropped from his grasp.

Hannigan braced his weight on his left foot, kicked out his right and swept it back hard against the crook of the Indian's knee. Aaron Darkwolf left his feet, hit the floor flat on his back.

Hannigan booted the knife across the room. Darkwolf recovered almost instantly, sprang back to his feet. Lunging at Hannigan, who was half-turned, he slammed into him at waist level, sent him stumbling into a table piled with skins.

He didn't hit it especially hard, but the table, rickety and strained with the weight of stacked skins, collapsed with a loud crash. Hannigan came down on the skins, some of which were still slick with blood. His hat flew from his head. He slipped as he tried get back to his feet, the skins as good as greased.

Darkwolf wasted no time coming down on top of him, did his best to pound Hannigan's brains out with a fist.

The blow ricocheted off the side of the manhunter's head, sent a cascade of stars exploding across his vision.

The Indian followed up by jamming fingers into Hannigan's throat and nearly every other soft spot within reach.

The man might have been inexperienced but he had a repertoire of painful holds and dirty fighting tactics.

Hannigan grabbed the man's wrist, twisted, heard a satisfying snap. Darkwolf let out a yowl.

Jerking up a knee, the manhunter buried it in the skinner's midriff. An explosion of air left Darkwolf's lungs, along with a string of curses.

The pause gave Hannigan the advantage he needed. With every inch of his rangy frame paining he couldn't let the fight go any further. He hammered a fist into the bundle of nerves beneath the Indian's arm. Darkwolf's right arm went dead, dangling at his side. Panicked, he tried to scramble back, but Hannigan crawled after him, grabbing a leg and flipping the man onto his stomach.

Darkwolf struggled, spittle gathering at the corners of his mouth. 'Goddamn whiteman! Leave me the hell alone!'

Hannigan banged a fist against the side of the Indian's head, silencing him. Perched atop Darkwolf, he jammed the man's face against the floor, yanked an arm behind his back. 'I came here lookin' to talk, you sonofabitch, but after this stunt you're number one on my list of suspects in those killin's. You got anything to say about them to convince me different you best do it now.'

The Indian let out an angry yell. 'Ain't that the way it always is for men with different skin? You're no better than the rest of this goddamn town. Blame the Injun.'

'Ain't skin color that's putting you there, it's because I got the notion you got a temper you can't control. You ever take that temper out on your girlfriend?'

Darkwolf ceased struggling, gasping for breath. 'Polly was . . . my girl. She . . . didn't see no skin color.'

'That why you took her money? That how you treat those who make you an equal?'

'What the hell business is it of yours? She was a whore. No one else would want her.'

'I'm sure you're quite a catch yourself. I reckon from the way you're all choked up with grief you told me just what your relationship with her was.'

'You don't know nothin' 'bout me. No one in this town does.'

'I reckon I know enough to tell me you ain't worth the skin the Good Lord put you in. Whether that makes you a killer or not is another thing. I aim to find out. You best hope the trail don't lead back to you or I won't waste my time bringing you in for a trial . . .'

Hannigan got off the man, backed towards the door. His muscles quivered from strain and sweat ran down his face. He ached in too many spots to count.

Darkwolf climbed to his feet. 'Get the hell out of here.' Fury blazed in his dark eyes. Hannigan wondered how many times Polly Maybrick had seen that very look, and if that was the thing that had frozen into her last sight the night she met her death.

'You remember what I said.' With that Hannigan wiped a forearm across his bleeding lip, then stooped to grab his hat, which lay near the door.

With a swish of clothing Hannigan straightened, his hand sweeping for his Peacemaker. The gun came up in a blur, leveled on Aaron Darkwolf as the man reached for his knife. The Indian froze, stooped, rage on his face.

'You reckon you're faster than a bullet, give it a try.'

The young man's eyes narrowed, but he made no

attempt to grab the knife.

The manhunter backed from the shack, closing the door behind him, at once more certain the man was a menace, but unconvinced that he was a whore-killer. Darkwolf couldn't control his temper, carried a heart full of hate, but was he the type who lurked in shadows, waiting to prey on vulnerable women?

From within the shack Hannigan heard an angry yell, then a loud thunk. Darkwolf had hurled the knife at the door. The Indian made no attempt to follow Hannigan, however.

A grim expression filtered onto Hannigan's face as he started back towards the main part of town. Frustration weevilled into his nerves. He'd managed to antagonize yet another person in this town but was still no closer to stopping a killer. Each of his suspects was fully capable of murder, yet at the same time not credible. Doc Francis's opinion of whores being a blight on society gave him a motive, but was it burning enough to send him on a gruesome crusade? Darkwolf and Pruitt profited from the women – where was their motive? Hannigan needed more than a bad temper before he could convict them.

The trouble was going to be getting a lead on a monster who hid in the darkness.

CHAPTER SIX

'Read all about it!' a boy yelled, running along the board-walk, a bundle of papers tucked beneath an arm and a single paper in his raised hand. ''Nuther whore killed in Gull's Court!'

Tootie spotted the boy as she stepped from the hotel. Her dress was a conservative powder-blue gingham, her hair hung straight and loose, her make-up had been scrubbed from her Mexicali-tinged features. Wouldn't do for Hannah Garret to appear anything but fresh-faced first thing in the morning, though how rested she looked was another matter.

The dark half-circles that nestled beneath her eyes told anyone who bothered to look that she hadn't slept most of the night. Racing, jumbled thoughts, bursts of jealousy over Hannigan's past with Catherine, as well as anxiety over their quarrel had all made her no less comfortable with the situation in the morning light and no less mind-weary. But the choice was no longer hers. She'd made her feelings plain enough. What came next was up to Hannigan. He needed to decide which trail he wanted to take and whether that trail included her. And he would have to do it soon. She wasn't about to compete with the ghosts of his past nor pry at secrets he refused to share. If he wanted her, he would have to give her something, anything, to indicate they had a future. She could give him time, then, but not like this, not when he wouldn't open up at all. The time had come to force a play, she reckoned. If he chose Catherine, then so be it. She wasn't about to beg any man. She had too much pride and promises weren't worth having if they weren't given freely.

She stepped from the boardwalk and crossed the street, cutting off the boy as he screamed the headlines again.

'Paper, miss?' he said.

'Didn't your mama ever tell you whore's a cuss word?' She said it with a glint in her eye and lilt in her voice, digging a coin out of the small change purse in her dress pocket.

The boy's face brightened. 'My mama swears worse than a drover, ma'am.'

Tootie laughed and handed him a coin, plus a penny extra. He grinned, passed her a paper, then scurried down the boardwalk, shouting the headlines over and over.

Tootie scanned the bold type, then the story detailing what had happened to Mary Ryan. Her stomach tightened and her heart dropped. Mary Ryan. 'Dammit . . .' she whispered, shaking her head. That was the gal she'd tried to warn off the street last night.

Her eyes widened suddenly as she read the next paragraph:

'. . . a note was received by this office, slipped under the door sometime during the night . . .'

Her lips parted in surprise. The newspaper owner had received a note from the killer? What kind of man butchered a woman then boasted publicly about it?

She read on, her gaze scrutinizing the contents of the letter, which the paper had reprinted in its entirety:

Dear Law
This one squealed a mite 'fore I kilt her but I had great fun
all the same. I kept the ear for myself. I will fry it in lard.
Sorry to deny the pigs but I left them the rest. Reckon I'll
keep on about my work until I have cleaned this town.
Even the new one won't catch me 'fore I finish. I wish him
luck trying. ha ha. Perhaps I shall leave him better
clues . . .

Tootie stopped reading and lifted her gaze from the paper to the newspaper office a few doors down. Was this letter some sort of sick joke, an effort to capitalize on the crimes to sell papers?

She folded the newspaper and strode down the boardwalk, determined to find out. Hannah Garret was a reporter, after all, and she reckoned it was time to start investigating the story.

Reaching the office, which boasted Miller's Pass *Ledger* in gilded letters across a large window, she grabbed the door-handle and twisted. She stepped inside and closed the door behind her. A smell, redolent of ink, assailed her nostrils. The room was dingy, with dusty streams of sunlight filtering through dirty windows. Peering about, she saw a long table holding rolled paper, a printing press and a board adorned with moveable type. A desk stood to the left, near a small side window, behind which sat a man with a longish face and brown wavy hair. He looked up from a pad, upon which he'd been scrawling, his eyes piercing her from beneath a green visor.

'Can I help you?' His voice was light, airy, almost femi-
nine.

'You the owner?' She stepped a few feet further into the
room.

The man stood, laying his pen on the desk, a peculiar
smile oiling his lips. A ladies' man, she pegged him for, or
one who at least saw himself as such. 'That's right. Arthur
Seckart's the name. And you are?'

'Hannah Garret. I'm a reporter for a newspaper up
Denver way. News about your murders got me assigned to
the story. They sent me down here to look into them.'

'They sent a woman?'

'It's the eighties, Mr Seckart.'

He laughed, and it annoyed her because it came with a
note of condescension, but she smiled a demure smile all
the same. 'Surprises me they'd send a gal when it's women
getting killed.'

She raised an eyebrow. 'I understood it was only certain
women being killed?'

He nodded. 'That's right, whores. So far. But who's to
say a fella who does this sort of thing's all that particular?'

Did something hide behind the way he said that? She
wasn't sure, but she aimed to prod him a bit. 'You know
any of these women personally, Mr Seckart?'

His face reddened and he said, 'No, of course not,' a bit
too quickly. He was lying. He knew one or all of the girls.
But accusing him of such wouldn't get her anywhere for
the moment. She could check his story with some of the
other gals at the saloon later to see if they could provide a
name for whichever girl he knew, if it had any relevance to
the case. At this juncture, it merely pegged him as more
weasely than she had at first believed, since he wore a band
on his finger.

107

'Did you write this story?' She tossed the newspaper in her hand on to the desk. 'The one about the killer?'

'Why, yes, I did.' Pride rode into his high-pitched voice.

'So you discovered the note the article tells of?'

'Found it on the floor when I came in this morning. Figure whoever left it did it during the night.'

His voice didn't waver and he looked her dead in the eye. He wasn't lying. 'Why do you think a fella like this killer would send a note to a newspaper?'

His face tightened a notch. 'You ain't askin' me if I hoaxed it, are you?'

While the thought had occurred to her, she'd dismissed it after concluding he was telling the truth about its discovery. 'Why, not for a moment, Mr Seckart.' Her smile warmed and she saw him relax. 'I just wonder why a killer would do such a thing. Why come out of the shadows and risk giving the marshal a lead?'

Seckart shrugged. 'I reckon he wanted to taunt the marshal, not give him a lead.'

'Seems it would just irritate him, doesn't it? Maybe make him more eager to catch a whore-killer than he might otherwise be? I mean, let's face it, Mr Seckart, whores don't make the top of most lawmen's list of priorities.'

'No, I reckon they don't. And I don't reckon the marshal gives a care about those girls.'

'Heard he sends the bodies to the doc, though. Maybe he cares some?'

Seckart laughed. 'He and the doc see eye to eye on the whore situation. Whatever reason he sends those bodies to the doc, it isn't because he gives a damn.'

'This note, you still have it?'

'Why, yes, I do. I planned on turning it over to the

marshal, for all the good it'll do. Imagine he'll be over soon enough, once he gets wind of the article.'

'May I see the note, Mr Seckart?' She came closer to him, making sure he could smell the perfume she wore, and folded her arms about herself, until her small bosom strained against her dress. She smiled as his gaze latched on to her front, almost laughed at how easy some men were to manipulate. If only Hannigan fell prey to her charms quite so easy.

'Mr Seckart?' she prodded.

'Huh?' His head jerked up and he grinned sheepishly. 'Oh, yes, the note.' He yanked open a desk drawer. For a moment she got a look at something else in the drawer: a number of loose sheets of paper that startled her enough to rattle her composure. He noticed as he pulled an envelope from the pile and handed it to her.

'Something wrong, Miss Garret?'

No point in trying to skirt it. 'Those drawings . . .'

Seckart nodded, reached into the drawer and pulled out the loose papers. He set them on the desk, fanning them out across the blotter. Three sketches, each showing the horribly mutilated body of a woman with exquisite detail. 'The murder victims. I'm something of an amateur artist. The marshal let me sketch the bodies before he sent them to the doc. Pretty good, don't you think?'

She nodded, because in fact they were, but his eagerness for her approval and lack of emotion where the mutilated corpses were concerned made her wonder whether maybe there weren't a darker side to this man.

'You published these in your paper?' She looked away from the drawings, which disturbed her more than she would have admitted to anyone.

'The first one I did. Plan to publish them as a series.

Didn't get to draw Mary Ryan, but maybe I can find a model and piece it together from the doc's description.'

She nodded a slight nod, the expression on her face mirroring the queasiness in her belly. Those women might have been whores but she saw publishing their naked, mutilated likenesses for all the town to see as disrespectful to their memory. Sometimes the press went too far, in her estimation.

She turned her attention to the envelope in her hand and pulled out the letter, which was penned on a type of parchment and folded in half. Upon opening it, she noted the scrawly handwriting, done in red ink. The ink was blotchy in places, as if the killer – assuming he had indeed written it – had paused, thinking over his next words. The newspaper had reprinted it word for word. She placed the letter back in the envelope, then passed it back to Seckart.

'Thank you, Mr Seckart. I think I've got a good start for my story. I may contact you if I think of something else?'

'Why, certainly, Miss Garret. I'd be obliged.' His smile resembled the expression of a fox about to eat a chicken. He replaced the letter and sketches in the drawer. She picked up her newspaper, went to the door, then clutched the handle.

'Ah, Miss Garret . . .'

She turned, seeing his gaze rake the length of her body. 'Yes, Mr Seckart?'

'Would you be interested in doing some modeling for me? I'm doing figure studies for a book I hope to publish. I think you'd be perfect for it. Perhaps you wouldn't mind coming to my office one evening . . .'

A lecherous glint betrayed his intent. She gave him a honey-coated smile. 'Why, Mr Seckart, I'm flattered, but if

I recall figure models aren't wearing a stitch in those books.'

'Why, um, no, but it's strictly an artistic endeavor.'

'I'm certain it is, Mr Seckart, but I'm far too modest a girl. Perhaps one of the gals at the saloon . . .' She winked and left the office, wishing she could spend the next hour in a bath scrubbing the feeling of filth off her skin.

As she closed the door and turned, she saw a man standing on the boardwalk. He was dressed in a dark suit and a tin star glinted in the sunlight.

'Who are you?' He took a step towards her. A challenge laced his voice, as if he disliked her for no reason.

'Why, you must be the marshal.' She forced her voice to remain steady, judging she wouldn't be able to manipulate this man the way she had Seckart.

'You didn't answer my question.'

'My name's Hannah Garret. I'm a reporter from Denver. I came here to write a story about the women who were murdered in this town.'

His face remained emotionless. 'They weren't women, they were whores. Probably best if you went back to Denver and forgot about it.'

'Why, I can't do that, Marshal. Not after the killer sent a letter to the paper promising more killings.' She didn't like the man and she didn't know why. Her intuition was working overtime, though her strained nerves and lack of sleep might have accounted for it.

The marshal nodded. 'Stupid bastard's going to have the whole town in an uproar.' His gaze narrowed, and he peered more closely at her. 'Have we met somewhere?'

A bolt of apprehension sizzled through her. He had been in the saloon last night. Had he noticed Tootie, the bargirl? She felt certain he had, but it was her job to keep him from connecting that girl with Hannah Garret. 'I'm sure we've never met, Marshal.'

'I am not so sure. I do not forget a face. It will come to me, but I've seen you somewhere.'

She noticed his accent growing thicker, wondered if it had to do with his level of agitation. 'I'm sure you're mistaken, Marshal. I would remember you.'

He didn't take his gaze off her and she felt the need to get out from under that stare. 'As I said, it will come to me.'

'Good day, Marshal.' She stepped past him, wanting to give him no more time to think on it. For a moment she worried that he might reach out and stop her. But he didn't.

She headed back to the hotel, the letter having told her nothing more than that whoever sent it enjoyed murder and had decided to make a game of it. One other thing she felt certain of: the 'new one' meant Jim Hannigan; the killer knew he was here to bring him down. Did he know about her as well? A sneaking suspicion told her he did, in one of her guises or the other. Perhaps he had seen her at the hotel or the saloon. Whatever the case, she needed to double her guard. A mistake this time could prove deadly.

Bertrand Mitre watched the dark-haired woman enter the hotel. The same girl who had ridden in with Hannigan, then split off to ride in alone. He knew the reason they were here now, though he was surprised Hannigan had taken on a partner. He had figured the manhunter for a loner.

That girl . . .

He had seen a bargirl leave the saloon last night, dark-haired, wearing a lot of make-up, walking normally until she reached the hotel. Then she had gone into an act, pretended to be drunk. He had given little thought to that, but now it suddenly made sense. They were the one and the same, this woman today and that whore last night. She had gussied herself and acted in a different manner, but they were the same person. Mitre laughed under his breath, satisfied with himself for figuring it out. Grabbing her would be easy work now that he knew her secret.

'Your debt's come due, Hannigan,' he whispered. He edged back into the side-street, then headed for a spot just outside town where he'd made camp. 'Tonight . . .'

CHAPTER SEVEN

Hannigan downed a cup of Arbuckle's, then poured another from the steaming pot next to his hat on the table. Few patrons occupied tables at the café, most having filtered out after the noon rush. The place was small, but bright, with blue-checkered table cloths, and the aromas of strong coffee, fresh-baked apple pie and sizzling beef-steak. He'd ordered a piece of the pie but had only poked at it, having little appetite, with the image of the murdered girl invading his mind and the memory of the stench at the animal skinner's shack still lingering in his nostrils.

You're getting soft, he told himself. He'd seen plenty of gruesome things in his time, but in this instance he felt as though someone had shown him visions of hell, of what real evil did when it walked the earth. He wasn't a religious man but these murders made him wonder whether demons didn't inhabit the bodies of some men and cause them to commit heinous acts. The notion augmented his worry over Tootie and Catherine, the danger they placed themselves in. Either was a target for a monster who slaughtered whores.

Motion at the corner of his eye brought him from his thoughts and he looked up to see Tootie in a gingham dress standing beside the table, a newspaper tucked beneath her arm.

'Mind if I sit down, Mr Hannigan?'

He peered at her, surprise on his face. 'Suit yourself, Miss . . .'

'Garret, Hannah Garret. I'm a reporter from Denver.' She said it loud for the benefit of anyone who might be eavesdropping. She slid onto a seat, her mahogany eyes weary. Hannigan knew that weariness was his responsibility.

He lowered his voice. 'How'd you know I was here?'

'You weren't in your room. I checked around with some of the townsfolk. Apparently your reputation's gotten around quick. Didn't take long to find a fella who had seen you come in here. He also said he saw you lookin' around some street.'

'I took a look at the other murder scenes, but the killer left no trail. He must have wiped any blood off on the girls' garments. Snuck into the saloon upstairs, too, by way of an outside stairway. Plenty of bloodstains in the room, but nothing else.'

She nodded, frowning. 'Usually the ones half this messy aren't this clever.'

His gaze avoided her eyes. 'Thought you wouldn't be talkin' to me after . . . last night.'

'Far as I know we still work together, don't we?' She said it with a certain coldness that made his innards clutch. He liked the warmth of her voice, the musical quality it had when she laughed. The coldness said she was wounded and it was deep. He'd seen it building since Revelation Pass. He knew a point would come that, when passed, a door would close to him. Maybe he'd already reached it. He should have been certain, but figuring emotional turning points wasn't his strong suit.

He should have told her he was sorry. That might have changed things. But his pride got in the way. 'Coffee?' he asked instead, cursing himself for the sonofabitch he was capable of being.

She nodded without much enthusiasm, sighed, then tugged the newspaper from beneath her arm and set it on the table. 'You've read it?'

'Yeah.' He said. He signaled the waitress to bring another cup, then filled it after she departed.

'He knows you're after him.'

His gaze drifted out the window. Folks passed by in the midday street; a buckboard rattled past. 'Reckon he's taunting me.'

'What kind of man does this? What kind of man mocks the law after butchering women this way?'

'Outlaws are a cocky lot. They get full of themselves, like to brag. That's usually when I catch them. Reckon this fella has some of the same blood.'

'I questioned the newspaper owner.' She sipped at her coffee, then added: 'He didn't know any more than the article said.'

'You get a look at the note?' He didn't turn away from the window. He was having trouble looking her in the eye. It was only making matters worse, but he struggled with his emotions and didn't want her reading them; she was far too good at that.

'Written in red ink, in a hand that looked like child's scrawl.'

'No chance the newsman did it to create a sensation?'

'I'd lay bet he didn't, but he's got some gruesome drawings of the dead women in his drawer, so maybe he's a better liar than I want to give him credit for.'

'Drawings?' He looked at her, curiosity on his face.

With a nod, she took another sip of her coffee. 'He's an artist, wants to publish them as a book.'

'Peculiar ambition.'

She nodded. 'You talk to the Indian? He say anything?'

'He said plenty, most of it blue. Tried to cut me into little pieces, too.'

Concern jumped into her eyes, chasing away some of the coldness. 'That makes him look right suspicious.'

Hannigan nodded noncommittally. 'He's got a temper . . . something scrawled on a wall near the murder scene this morning seems to indicate he was responsible, but I reckon that's what someone wants me to think. It's too convenient.'

'But he tried to kill you. Might have done the same to his woman.'

'But would he kill her in such a brutal way? She was turning her money over to him. Why kill the goose that lays the golden eggs? And why kill the others?'

'Pruitt takes most of the girls' money. You ask me, he's the number one guy to be lookin' at.'

He shrugged. 'Same story with him. The girls give him money. A bastard all the way around, but a butcher? I dunno.'

'And the doc?' She raised an eyebrow.

'Been here a spell, could get his specimens in other-ways. Still, he's got a healthy dislike for Indians and whores.'

'So we got four suspects, if you include the newspaper owner, all without any real motive.'

'That's what it boils down to.'

' 'Course, any one of them could have just gone loco.'

'Never met a loco man this calculating.'

'Sure wouldn't call him normal.'

'Reckon not. One thing's for sure, he isn't likely to stop killing . . .'

She peered at him, a frown creasing her brow. His voice had betrayed something and she caught it.

'You might as well not go any further. It's my fault that gal last night got killed. I could have gone after her, made her get off the street. I'm not backing off this case, no matter how dangerous. I owe her memory that much. And I can take care of myself.'

'Tootie . . .' He dragged out her name.

'Hannah,' she said. 'Don't want to blow my cover, do we?'

'It might not matter. This killer knows I'm here. He might have connected us.'

'Don't see how.'

'Ain't taking any chances. I'm askin' you as a favor, please ride back and wait for me.'

'You don't honestly think that will work, do you?'

'I was hopin' . . .' He sighed, watching her stand, then lean over the table.

'I won't leave you here on your own, Jim. You've been makin' your share of mistakes lately and I've got your back till . . .' Her words trailed into a whisper. 'Till you don't want that anymore.' She straightened, but he saw it in her eyes: it was Catherine. She might well have said till he made a choice between her and the auburn-haired woman.

'Where you goin'?' he asked, having no desire to press the matter.

'I'm a reporter. I'll ask around about the murders, see if we've missed anything.'

'You're making yourself a target.'

'Am I?'

He didn't like the smile she gave him as she walked away.

She was a stubborn woman, damn her exquisite hide. For all the times he found that trait endearing there were just as many it drove him nuts. This was one of the latter. He supposed he was old-fashioned, wanting to protect her when she didn't really need protecting. Having a man take care of her wasn't something she cottoned to, unless it came reciprocated. She could protect herself better than most any man, but, for him, accepting that was as easy as teaching a horse to talk. And this situation wasn't exactly like their normal cases.

That's an excuse, an inner voice told him. Wouldn't matter if he were chasing down a schoolmarm wielding a wicker basket, it would be the same. He was just denying the obvious – his feelings had grown to a point he could no longer bury them.

An exaggeration, he assured himself, but accurate enough. If that woman was stubborn, he had her beat by a long country trail.

As he entered the hotel, the clerk motioned to him, drawing him from his thoughts.

'Mr Hannigan, a package arrived for you.' The clerk reached beneath the counter and brought out a paper-wrapped box about six inches long and eight wide. He set it atop the counter.

An alarm went off in Hannigan's mind, as he approached the desk. No one but his secretary knew he was here and he wasn't likely to be sending packages.

'Where'd it come from?' Hannigan surveyed the package, which was tied with string and unaddressed, except for his name and the word 'hotel' scrawled in red ink on the outside.

The clerk shrugged. 'Dunno. Horance at the telegraph office said he found it sitting on his desk when he got back from lunch. Since it had your name and we're the only hotel he brought it here. Glad to get rid of it to be honest. Whoever sent it to you must have mailed perishables, because something sure ain't daisy-fresh.'

A dark dread brewed in his mind. He grabbed the string and snapped it with a sharp tug. Unwrapping the paper revealed a box with a reddish brown stains soiling the top. As he pried back the flaps a foul odor wafted from within.

'Jesus . . .' he whispered, his belly sinking. He closed the box before the clerk got a look at what was inside.

'Everything all right, Mr Hannigan?' The clerk's nose scrunched. 'That sure smells powerful awful.'

'Like you said, someone mailed perishables . . .' He picked up the box, then headed back towards the door.

Once outside, he drew a deep breath and made his way to the doctor's office. He entered and went to the examination room.

The examination table was empty and the doctor was just seeing out a patient, a young woman. The woman gave Hannigan a smile, but Francis acknowledged his presence with a scowl.

'I already did what you asked, Hannigan.' Francis leaned against the examination table. 'She's getting her burial. You didn't have to come back to threaten me again.'

Hannigan walked over to the table and set down the box. 'This is what I came for.'

The doctor looked at him, then the box. 'Something spoiled?'

'You might say that. Take a look.'

The doctor opened the flaps and peered into the box. 'I see . . .' His expression didn't change.

'What is it?'

'Why, I'd say it's a kidney. And here I thought I was the only one interested in specimens.'

'I got a notion this belongs to that girl you had in here earlier.'

The doctor nodded, then went to his counter and selected a jar. Within the jar was a human kidney in preservative fluid. The doctor held the jar near the box, comparing the contents of both. 'I'd say there's an excellent chance you're right, Mr Hannigan. Both are in the same stages of Bright's disease, both the same size approximately, though, of course, this one in the box looks as if it was lying about for a few hours.' The doctor set the jar on the table. 'Where'd you get it?'

'Someone sent it to me. Apparently someone who thinks he's playing some sort of sick game with me.'

'You don't bring out the best in folks.' The doctor smiled, but the expression missed the mark.

Hannigan took the parcel and was about to close the flaps. He paused, noticing a slip of paper sticking to an inside wall, coated with brown smears. He pulled the slip from the box, a folded three-by-four piece of parchment paper. He opened the parchment and he studied the scrawled red-ink words:

From Hades
Mister Hannigon
I send you the kidney I took this marning. I thought you
might like it back. It spoiled so I could not eat it the way I
planned. Next time I shall send you something larger,

perhaps a hand? Perhaps from your woman?
  Bring me in when you can Mr Hannigon

'What's it say?' the doctor asked, curiosity on his face.

'It says the man we're dealing with is one sick sono-fabitch I best catch yesterday.' Hannigan folded the note and stuffed it into his shirt pocket. He closed the box, picked it up.

He left the doctor staring after him with a puzzled look on his face.

Jim Hannigan shoved open the door to the marshal's office and stepped inside. Agitation crawled through his nerves. He didn't like being toyed with and whoever this killer was, he held the advantage. He knew who Hannigan was and had a facility at hiding in plain sight. But the risk to himself little concerned him. It was the note's mention of 'his woman' that set him on edge. Either the killer had pierced Tootie's disguise or had seen him talking to Catherine the night he arrived. Neither possibility reassured him, but his money was on Tootie. Somehow the killer had figured her out.

The marshal sat behind his desk, looking over the morning paper, his gaze focused on the article about the letter sent by the killer. He looked up at Hannigan with no pleasure. 'What the hell do you want?'

Hannigan dropped the box on to the desk. He fished the note from his pocket, tossed it beside the parcel.

'What's that?' The marshal's eyes narrowed.

'A kidney from the girl who was killed last night.' Hannigan held his voice level, though worry made that a struggle.

The marshal didn't register any emotion. 'How'd you

come by it?'

'The sonofabitch sent it to me. Left it at the telegraph office without being seen.'

The marshal glanced at the box, then folded his paper and dropped it on the desk. He picked up the note. After reading it he refolded the missive and tossed it back on the desk.

He cocked an eyebrow, his blue eyes hard. 'What do you want me to do about it?'

'Your job. That should prove this threat's serious enough to deputize a few men and have them patrol the streets at night. Wire the county marshal, have him send some men down to help.'

'You saying you can't handle this fellow?' Hannigan caught a taunt in the marshal's voice he damn well didn't like.

'That note threatens someone I care about. I won't take chances with her life.'

'Who?'

'A woman I work with. She came in with me. The killer likely knows that somehow.'

A light danced in the lawdog's eyes. 'This woman, her name Hannah Garret by any chance?'

Hannigan supposed there was no harm in admitting it now that the killer had threatened Tootie. 'She's my partner.'

The marshal nodded, a slight smile oiling his lips. 'And this partner of yours, she plays saloon whore at night?'

Hannigan peered at the man, taken by surprise. The lawdog was smarter than he had given him credit for, if lazy. 'Her life's in danger and she's too stubborn to listen to reason.'

'Way I see it, she takes her chances working with a fella

like you.' The marshal straightened in his chair and leaned both forearms on the desk. 'Won't be needin' no men patrolling, though. Already have the killer in custody.'

'What?' It wasn't often Hannigan was caught totally off guard, but it happened for the second time in the space of seconds. 'What the hell do you mean, you have him?'

The marshal ducked his chin towards the back, to a row of cells. Hannigan's gaze followed. In the first cell a man sat on the edge of a bunk, forearms across his knees, a sneer on his dark face. Aaron Darkwolf said nothing, merely glared at Jim Hannigan with fury in his eyes.

Hannigan looked back to the marshal. 'What's he doin' in there?'

'Like I said, he's the killer?'

'Based on what?' Hannigan's brow furrowed.

'Based on the fact I caught him sneaking out of Polly Maybrick's boarding-house room with a bloody piece of cloth in his pocket.

'When?'

' 'Bout half an hour ago.'

Hannigan looked back to the cell, doubt swimming in his mind. 'That true?' he asked Darkwolf.

The half-breed's sneer widened. 'I got a note telling me Polly left me some money in her room. I went to fetch it.'

'What about the bloody cloth?'

A look of worry invaded the man's eyes. 'I told the marshal already. I saw it lying there on the bed and figured someone would find a way to blame me for it, so I took it. Was gonna burn it.'

'That sounds flimsy as hell, Darkwolf.' Yet a curious indignation in the man's eyes told Hannigan he might be telling the truth.

The Indian shrugged. 'Don't matter. Innocent or guilty they hang Injuns, don't they?'

Hannigan studied him, looking for any indication the man was lying. 'What about this note you claim you got? Still have it?' Hannigan entertained the notion that he could compare the writing with the one sent to him with the kidney.

Darkwolf nodded. 'Left it right on the table in my shack.'

Hannigan looked back to the marshal, who shook his head.

'Searched his place,' said Severin. 'No note anywhere. He's lying.'

'The hell I am!' Darkwolf swung his feet up, lay on the bunk, and fixed his gaze to the ceiling.

'You best still deputize some men, Marshal. I ain't so sure you got the right man.'

The marshal laughed. 'Mr Hannigan, whatever would I do without you to tell me my job?'

'All sounds a might pat, doesn't it? Mysterious note sends him to Polly's room where he just happens to find a piece of bloody cloth? She wasn't killed in her room. Why would that cloth be there? And why would he have left it that night, then decided to remove it now?'

'Who knows why that kind does anything? Caught him red-handed, if you will pardon the expression, where he's concerned. His note story didn't hold up. He had plenty of time to send you that box, too, and you know how sneaky those Injuns are.'

Hannigan saw the marshal had made up his mind. He wouldn't budge and maybe he was right. Maybe he was reaching for inconsistencies in his worry over Tootie. He glanced at Darkwolf again, wondering whether the man was indeed the killer and why. It still made no sense to him. What motive could he have with the other girls?

'I got a notion you're making a mistake, Marshal. I been at this long enough to see through smoke.'

'Then perhaps it is time you should retire? Buy yourself a nice farm somewhere and raise sheep. Perhaps your woman would like that, yes?' Severin's accent strengthened with the sarcasm.

Hannigan could barely restrain himself from reaching over the desk and throttling the man. Lord knew he wanted to. He hadn't liked the marshal from the moment he met him and nothing had happened since to change that opinion. He turned and went to the door, grabbing the handle.

'Hey, are you not taking your present?' he heard the marshal ask behind him in an annoyed tone. 'It smells mighty bad.'

'Keep it.' Hannigan pulled open the door. 'Reckon it ain't the only thing stinking in here.'

CHAPTER EIGHT

Hannigan had spent the past hour before dusk running Aaron Darkwolf's story about going to Polly Maybrick's room over and over in his mind. He'd decided to ignore the marshal's word and have himself a look around Darkwolf's shack, but discovered that Severin wasn't lying when he said there was no note to be found. Yet why would Darkwolf murder his girlfriend and three others? Crime of passion, anger, might explain Polly's death, but what connection did the other three women have? Did the half-breed just hate so much it twisted his mind into committing such acts? If so, why leave a clue to himself on a wall and in Polly's room? Would he risk sneaking a box into a telegraph office and leaving a note for the newspaper? Taunt the law? He was an animal skinner, true, and would probably have enough knowledge to locate and remove an organ, but something about the whole thing just wasn't settling in Hannigan's craw. It seemed too tidy, though he'd seen outlaws make stupider mistakes and leave trails to their crimes.

He stepped from the hotel into the warm night air. Dusk had turned to purple shadows and amber ghosts cast from lanterns. He'd checked Tootie's room a few moments ago, finding her either not there or not wanting to answer his knock.

If she was out, he reckoned he'd find her at the saloon. Maybe if he told her about the threat in the note he'd be able to persuade her to leave the case to him.

You really think you got a chance in Hell of that, Hannigan?

He was only foolin' himself if he did. She'd give him the same answer she had earlier. He considered telling her the killer was caught, convincing her of something he didn't believe himself, that Darkwolf was guilty. Send her back while he cleaned up the details.

You're talking about tricking her, Hannigan. You saw how well that worked out in Revelation Pass . . .

Judas Priest, wasn't anything ever easy?

He crossed the dusty street to the opposite boardwalk, headed towards the saloon. The sounds of music and laughter from the drinkerie echoed into the darkening night.

A woman suddenly came from the shadows beyond the saloon.

He stopped, peering at her. 'Catherine . . .'

'I wanted to talk to you away from Pruitt. I knew you'd come back tonight.'

He sighed. 'When I told you to try to keep the girls off the street, I was including you.'

She laughed, an airy sound. 'Haven't you heard? The marshal caught the man who did it. Polly's boyfriend.'

'Not so sure about that.'

She took a step closer and the scent of her perfume made his head want to spin. In the light bleeding from the saloon she looked entrancing. Her smooth shoulders and ripe bosom accentuated by a green sateen bodice were enough to drive any man out of his head with passion. Her full lips and hazel eyes threatened to draw him in, leave him drowning in her soul. 'I don't want this anymore, Jim. This life, I mean. I want to go back to what we were, start over.'

'Catherine . . .'

'Shhh . . .' She placed a finger to his lips. A shiver of arousal skittered through his belly and feelings from the past welled up and threatened to overcome him. 'We can go back to the way it was before you left. I know what I am and I know what you are. A whore and killer. Neither of us has been perfect, but that all doesn't matter anymore. Now that your job's done nothing's holding us back from being together.'

'When I left you that day I told you this was no life for a woman. I told you I couldn't just settle down, and that I couldn't get close to anyone.'

'But you never told me why.' Her eyes searched his and his resistance wavered. That never would have happened those years ago, never would have happened before . . .

Tootie . . .

'Things haven't changed, Catherine.'

'I know about her, Jim.'

'What?' His belly tightened.

'I saw the way she looked at you in the saloon. I saw you look at her. She didn't just show up here lookin' for a job out of the blue and she isn't any whore. She got away with it for a night but it won't be long before Jack's on to her.'

'She's good at her job . . .' he whispered, searching for words. Things were getting out of hand. Too many folks had made the connection between them and that made their business riskier than it already was.

'She's more than that. She's in love with you.' Catherine bowed her head, then looked back to him. 'But are you in love with her? Do you love her more than you loved me?'

'I never—'

'Said it? I know. You couldn't, but I was willing to wait. I'm willing to give you all the time you need to say it now. Just take me out of here. Please. Take me somewhere I can forget the things I've done, where I can be clean and safe this time.' She suddenly lifted to her tiptoes and placed her lips to his.

Tootie slid back into the shadows a street down from the saloon. She'd heard Hannigan knock on her door a short time ago, but exhaustion and emotion had overcome her after talking with him at the café and she'd fallen into a fitful sleep. By the time his tapping registered and she'd reached the door he was already starting down the stairs to the lobby. She'd hastily packed herself into her whore get-up and sneaked out through a side-window on to an outside stairway, only to come upon the scene outside the saloon.

She pressed her back to the wall of a building, tears welling in her eyes, running. Goddammit, she didn't cry. Not she. But emotion burned in her throat and hurt surged in her being like a firebrand.

She had seen Catherine place her lips to his.

I've lost . . .

The words drummed in her mind, a dirge. She'd held to the silly notion she could reach him, draw him out from whatever kept him from telling her what he felt for her. Maybe it was never there. Maybe she had simply imagined it, built it up in her mind to be something it wasn't, until it could wound her deeper than anything had since the day she lost her parents.

'You're a fool . . .' she whispered, forcing the tears back. She wrapped her arms about herself, a sob shuddering through her. She saw nothing ahead now, nothing but loneliness and a return to a life with the agency she'd left the day she'd teamed with Jim Hannigan.

Maybe there's still a chance . . .

Was she fooling herself again by telling herself Catherine had forced herself on Hannigan? Would he be any more likely to give Catherine what he hadn't given her? Three words and a commitment to a life shared?

The thought suddenly died in her mind. Someone clutched at her in the darkness. A small sound of surprise escaping her lips, she reacted instantly, tried to kick backward at whoever locked an arm about her waist, but hit nothingness. The move, however, likely prevented her throat from being sliced. A searing pain pierced her shoulder as she struggled. Then warm liquid, flowing down the front of her bodice. She'd been cut and a flashing thought cascaded though her mind. She had made another mistake, losing herself in misery, making herself vulnerable to someone sneaking up on her. In the shadows no one saw her, knew she was there . . . except someone stalking her, someone who murdered women of the line. No matter that she was only playing a part. The mistake had put her an inch away from death.

She struggled, trying to wrench free of his hold. His right hand was at her shoulder, with a knife, and she tried to twist away from it, partly successful. She spun half-around, able to see only the merest outline of a man, not much taller than herself.

Letting instinct and training take over, she kicked, hoping to nail a shin or kneecap. A grunt came from her attacker and she followed with a punch aimed at the

131

center of the blob of darkness before her. Her fist collided with his chest with a solid thud that nearly broke her wrist. Pain skewered her fingers and forearm.

The attacker didn't miss a beat. He tried to jam a hand over her mouth. She bit at the hand and let out an ear-splitting screech.

'Hannigan!' He was close enough to hear it, assuming he still stood in front of the saloon.

Ignoring the pain in her hand, she beat at the figure, hitting him over and over, fearful that any second a knife she couldn't see would plunge into her chest and end her life.

Please don't let me die before I tell him I love him . . .

It was a stupid thought, given what she'd seen a moment before, but the only one that meant anything to her.

She managed to break free, but a fist clonked her on the side of the face and she staggered back. Her senses spinning, her legs went out from under her, and she came down on her rear. Through the thunder in her mind, she heard her attacker's footsteps retreating down the side street. Her screech had scared him off. Toppling sideways, her face slammed into the ground. Dirt got into her mouth. Her heart banged against her ribs. She heard footsteps again, this time approaching.

'Please, Catherine, don't.' Jim Hannigan pushed Catherine back, the taste of her kiss lingering on his lips and old feelings churning in his heart. But something else rose above that: Tootie's face, her eyes, and an overwhelming feeling for her that rushed to the surface the moment Catherine's lips met his.

'You can't tell me you didn't feel anything, Jim.' Her

eyes widened with hurt and surprise. Maybe she had become a woman unused to men rejecting her, maybe she had become someone he no longer knew. They had been much younger when they met. Too young. Too much time and circumstance had trickled away since those days.

A screech calling his name stopped anything he might have said. He recognized Tootie's voice, but had never heard such desperation lacing it. An instant later he stepped past Catherine, bolting in the direction from which the scream had come. His hand swept for his Peacemaker; he had it out and finger ready on the trigger in one blurred fluid motion.

His heart thudded as he reached the side street. He paused and listened. 'Tootie?' he called, muscles tense, sweat springing out on his brow. If anything happened to her . . .

'Jim . . . down here . . .' he heard her say. Her voice was weak, just ahead in the darkness. He entered the shadows, his senses alert for any sound of an attacker, the rustle of clothing, a clutched breath. Nothing but Tootie's ragged breathing. He edged forward, eyes adjusting somewhat to the darkness so he could pick out dim shapes.

He found her a few feet on, and knelt. 'Are you—'

'Yeah, he ran off.' Her voice came stronger, and he reckoned she was more frightened than hurt. He holstered his gun and helped her to her feet, then guided her out into the light of the main street. A gash in her shoulder leaked blood, which had soaked the fringe of her blue bodice.

Catherine came up beside them, worry on her face, her eyes concerned. 'What happened?'

Hannigan glanced at her but said nothing, because he noticed a man coming towards them from across the street.

'Marshal . . .' he said. His tone was cold.

Severin stopped before them, eyeing both girls then Hannigan, frowning. 'You're just a magnet for trouble, aren't you?'

Hannigan's tone leveled. 'Looks like maybe you got the wrong man in your jail, after all, doesn't it, Marshal? 'Less you let him out and didn't tell anyone.'

Severin's face darkened. 'No, he's still there.'

'Then I suggest you set him free, because he isn't the man you want.'

The marshal shrugged. 'Reckon I'll hold him just the same, until we're certain. This might have been a random attack.'

'You don't really believe that?' Hannigan couldn't keep the annoyance from his voice.

Severin didn't answer, instead looked at Tootie and Catherine a second time. 'Two women, Hannigan? You must be quite a man.'

Hannigan passed Tootie to Catherine. 'Get her to the doc's. Tell him he better treat her or I'll pay him a visit he won't appreciate.'

Catherine nodded, put an arm around Tootie and guided her away. The wound wasn't serious, though it would need treatment so that infection didn't set in, but mostly Hannigan just wanted Tootie and Catherine out of harm's way.

'Where you going?' Tootie asked, looking back over her shoulder, worry in her eyes.

'I'm going after the man who attacked you. Maybe the marshal wants to do the same?'

Severin raised an eyebrow. 'I still am not convinced the right man isn't in a cell. But I'll leave this one to you, Hannigan, since you're so eager to be useful. Maybe you'll earn that reputation of yours. I'll see the girls to Francis's place.'

Hannigan nodded, not about to spend any time arguing with him. He drew his gun and went into the side-street, crouching and sticking close to the wall of a building. He spent the next hour searching for any sign of the assailant, but whoever attacked Tootie had gotten clean away.

The lack of a trail frustrated him. He might have had a chance had he gone after the man immediately but his concern for Tootie had allowed precious minutes to give the attacker too big a head start. Tracking him in the dark would prove impossible. There were too many places to hide, too many doorways he might have ducked into.

The attack told him one thing for certain: no matter what Severin thought, the man in his cell was no longer on the suspect list. Someone else was responsible for the murders. That left Pruitt, Francis, the newspaper-owner or someone completely unknown. Hannigan figured he could scratch the doc off the list the moment he treated Tootie's wounds, if he were in his office. Francis had no way of doubling back to his office in time. Hannigan would have seen him.

The newspaperman was unlikely, too, since Hannigan noticed a light on in the office before he had gone after the killer, though he supposed the man could have snuck out by a back way. He couldn't cross him off the list quite yet.

That left Jack Pruitt or an unknown entity. Pruitt was off the hook if he was at the saloon and that was easy enough to determine. Hannigan walked down the boardwalk, paused outside the drinkerie, then stepped through the batwings. Scanning the room, he spotted the bar-owner behind the counter, giving him a look of pure murder.

Hannigan threaded his way through the tables to the bar, his gun suddenly in his hand. He was in no mood for another go-around with Pruitt and the man was going to answer questions whether he cared to or not.

'What the hell?' Pruitt's look of murder turned to annoyed surprise.

'How long you been here?'

'Since this afternoon.'

'You prove that?'

'Hell, yes, ask any of the girls or the folks in here.'

Hannigan would have laid bet the man was telling the truth. The manhunter saw no guilt in the man's eyes, only meanness.

Hannigan holstered his gun. 'I find out you're lying I'll be back. You best hope that doesn't happen.'

Pruitt glared but didn't move. Hannigan left the saloon and headed for the hotel. Tootie would be back by now and he reckoned he was in for a long night awake, listening, to make sure no one tried to attack her again. The attack proved that whoever lurked in the shadows knew her identity and her association with Hannigan.

That left him with no real suspects and a killer with an advantage Hannigan damn well didn't care for.

Catherine Tretlow walked Tootie back to the hotel after they left Doc Francis's office. The marshal had seen them there, but left shortly after. The doc had patched Tootie's shoulder, likely only because he feared the consequences if he did not.

A few jealous pangs had stabbed Catherine, watching the girl get fixed up. If that killer had gotten her, then she wouldn't have had to worry about competition for

Hannigan's affections, would she?

She scolded herself for the thought, knowing she really didn't want the girl to meet such a fate, but she knew the moment she kissed Hannigan that she had lost to the dark-haired beauty. Things were no longer the way they had been in the past. Perhaps they never had been. She'd merely deluded herself with a fantasy to keep herself going, to fan false hope. He had told her plain they had no future the day he left. But seeing him again . . . well, she had convinced herself maybe there was a chance.

But there was none. Whether he knew it or not his fate was entwined with that woman at the hotel and he loved her. It was only a matter of time before he realized it or did something stupid, like leaving, the way he had left her all those years ago.

Catherine wrapped her arms about herself, her high-laced shoes tapping hollowly on the boardwalk as she headed to the boarding-house where she had a room. The same boarding house in which Polly had lived.

A chill shuddered through her at the thought, but she didn't pay it much attention because a sound came from behind her. She whirled, searching the empty street. Somehow the shadows looked so sinister now, as if they could swallow her. She saw no one and told herself she had only imagined the sound. Still, she turned and hurried her step. The killer was still out there and had attacked one girl tonight. She wasn't about to give him a chance to make it two.

She reached the boarding house door a few moments later and rushed inside. She made her way down the dimly lit hallway, unlocked the door to her room and quickly shut it behind her.

She went to a table, ignited the kerosene lamp and shivered. The room was modest, with only a table and bed, a couple of hardback chairs and a small dresser for furniture.

Tears gathered in her eyes and she sobbed, resigning herself to being all she was now for the rest of her days. No man would want a whore. Everything she'd ever dreamed, everything she'd planned for her future was gone. It had melted away the moment she married that sonofabitch in Wolf's Bend. But, then, she never could tell when a man wasn't really in love with her, could she?

A rap on the door pulled her from her thoughts and she looked over to it. A sudden hope took hold, that Hannigan had felt the emotion in her kiss and had come back.

She ran to the door, placed her ear to it.

'Who is it?' she asked.

'Ma'am,' came a voice through the door. It was muffled but she thought she recognized it and her hope faded. He hadn't come back.

She pulled back the bolt and opened the door, gazing at the figure in the hallway.

'What's wrong? Has something happen—'

She wasn't able to finish the words before the knife flashed up and cut deep into her throat.

CHAPTER NINE

After making certain Tootie was safe in her room, Jim Hannigan spent a restless night dropping in and out of sleep. The memory of Catherine's kiss, the attack on Tootie and the lack of leads to the killer had all played hell with his mind.

Tootie had acted damn peculiar when he said good-night, distant, morose. At first he attributed it to their strained relationship and the fight from the night before, as well as the residual effects of the attack. But the more he dwelled on it the more he realized how she'd placed herself in a position to be assaulted by the killer. That wasn't like her and he saw only one reason for it: She had seen him and Catherine together outside the saloon, and if she had seen that she had seen Catherine kiss him. She might even have overheard their conversation.

So, a day later, he stared out the hotel window at the gathering dusk, wondering how everything had blown up in his face, but knowing he'd invited that very thing when he'd accepted this job. Thoughts of playing on a past relationship to make Tootie jealous had been juvenile, but damn, he had no practice with such things as relationships and the emotions that came with them. Still, that was no excuse.

He saw Tootie cross the street, then head towards the saloon. He had been planning on going there himself in a few moments. What he intended to do would be difficult, but he owed it to both women to set the record straight about what happened outside the saloon last night. Trouble was, one wasn't going to like it, but he couldn't let her think something existed where nothing did. The past was the past. Her kiss had stirred old feelings, arousal, but that was all. Anything he'd had with Catherine was over. He still cared about her, and he would do his damnedest to protect her, bring this killer down, but that was the most he could promise.

A sigh trickled from his lips. He wouldn't be surprised if they both told him to go to hell.

He'd spent most of the day chasing a ghost, scouring the street down which the killer had escaped in daylight. He found nothing. Too many footsteps had obliterated any chance of tracking the man.

The failure only frustrated him more. This wasn't his province. He tracked outlaws, not shadows. He was out of suspects, and it was likely only a matter of time before another girl met her death. He couldn't protect them all, nor persuade the marshal to expand his staff or call in help. Severin had remained stubborn, even obstinate, when Hannigan approached him a few hours ago. The lawdog insisted on keeping Darkwolf in jail, for his own protection, he'd said, though it was plain Darkwolf could not have attacked Tootie last night. Worse, Hannigan had witnessed a subtle shift in the town's demeanor. A handful of folks were getting antsy, vengeful, making noises about hanging the Indian for the crimes. The newspaper-owner, Seckart, hadn't helped matters when his morning edition carried an editorial pointing a finger squarely at the animal-skinner.

It was time. Dusk turned to darkness as if a shade had been drawn. Hannigan went to the bedpost and grabbed his Stetson, jammed it on his head.

The walk to the saloon felt like a march to the gallows. He had no wish to hurt Catherine again, had never intended to give her any indication he was here for anything more than to help a friend. He'd decided he would offer her whatever she needed to start a new life somewhere else, one that didn't involve selling herself. He doubted she would accept it but he had to try.

The saloon was in full swing and the moment he stepped through the batwings Jack Pruitt's face reddened and fury flashed in his eyes. His hand started for something beneath the counter, and Hannigan had no doubt it was a shotgun. The bar-owner was ready to get even; he wasn't going to rely on a blade and chance another disgraceful loss.

Hannigan's hand blurred as it liberated the Peacemaker from its holster. 'Don't!' he snapped and Pruitt stopped in mid-motion.

The manhunter walked towards the bar, while the patrons stared with mouths agape. Tootie, who stood at the end of the bar, froze with a puzzled expression.

'What the hell you doing back here?' Pruitt spat the words, spittle gathering at the edges of his mouth. 'Ain't you caused enough trouble? Get out 'fore I have the marshal run you out of town!'

'Be glad to – after I get what I came for.' Hannigan's gaze swept the saloon. 'Where is she?'

'Who?' Pruitt's hands came up and rested on the bartop. His bulky frame shook with rage, but he made no move for a weapon.

'Catherine, where is she?'

Tootie's face dropped and she leaned against the counter as if to keep herself from falling.

'Hasn't come in yet. Damn whore's late.'

'She ever late before?'

Pruitt shook his head. 'No. She won't be again neither, once I get . . .' He stopped, the look on the manhunter's face making him think better of whatever he'd been about to say.

Hannigan couldn't keep a plunging feeling out of his gut. He had no outward reason for it, but a dark suspicion crawled into his mind. 'Where's she live?'

Pruitt's face went a shade redder. 'What right you got comin' in here and—'

'Tell me!' Hannigan's voice jumped to a shout and he thumbed the hammer back. For one of the few times in his life his hand began to shake.

Jack Pruitt was a cruel man, but not a stupid one. Obviously he saw he was one trigger twitch away from winding up in the boneyard. His mouth made fish movements. 'She's . . . got a room at the boarding-house a couple blocks down, end of Cable Street. Number thirteen.'

Without a word, Hannigan backed from the saloon, keeping his aim on Pruitt until he got through the batwings.

Tootie sprang towards the batwings after him, a stricken look on her face.

'Where the hell you think you're going?' yelled Jack, starting around the bar.

Her hand plunged into her strawberry bodice top and brought out her derringer, leveling it on Jack until she reached the doors. He froze, face purple with rage by now.

142

'Wherever the hell I want. And if I hear you mistreat any of these girls again, I'll come back here and turn you into a girl, if you catch my meanin'.'

Her words carried to Hannigan out on the boardwalk but he didn't wait for her. He broke into a run, knowing she was following him down the boardwalk. As he reached the boarding-house at the end of Cable Street a few minutes later, dread geysered in his soul and his heart pounded in his throat.

You're jumping to conclusions, he assured himself. *She's just late. She's fine.*

Another voice told him he was dead wrong and what he'd find at the boarding-house would destroy every defense he'd built over the years to shield himself against the death he encountered in his work. Something told him no one, not even a man of vengeance, was prepared to face the utter human destruction a maniac like the one stalking Miller's Pass wrought.

He threw open the boarding-house door and stepped into a gloomy hallway. Gun still in hand, he brought it up close to his face and crept forward, his pulse thundering in his ears.

Please, don't let it be . . . Not her . . .

On reaching the door to number thirteen he stared at it a dragging instant, fear of what he'd find behind it freezing him in place. He swallowed hard, gun hand shaking again.

She's behind that door, Hannigan. You know it. You can feel it.

'No,' he whispered, voice quaking.

She's dead . . .

No, she's only lost track of time. That's all. He tapped on the door, keeping his gun near his face and moving off

143

to the side, back against the wall.

A sound from the hall jerked his head around. Tootie stood there, her face drawn, puzzled, perhaps even frightened. He'd never seen such a confusion of emotions on her.

He turned back to the door, tapped again. 'Catherine?' The name seemed to hang there, wavering, ghostly. He fought to control his voice, stop it from shaking. 'Catherine?' Louder this time.

No answer.

You're gonna feel like a fool if you bust in that door and she's just asleep . . .

He checked the handle and found it locked. He stepped back from the door and snapped a sharp kick. His boot-heel crashed into the wood above the lock.

As the wood splintered, the door bounded inward. He stopped it with a hand as it rebounded, shoved it open. The interior was pitch black; he could see nothing. He went back into the hall and grabbed one of the wall lanterns, lifted it from its mount.

With a deep breath, he returned to the room, holding the lantern out in front of him.

A rush of nausea surged into his belly. His legs trembled and cascades of heat washed through his face. Every emotion he'd struggled to suppress over his years as a manhunter when coming upon the scene of violent death came thundering through him in mind-spinning waves. His gun hand shook uncontrollably and the lanternlight jittered.

The room was a study in scarlet and nightmare. He'd never seen so much blood, so much carnage. Puddles of crimson gleamed with reflected lanternlight on the floors; scarlet smeared every wall and piece of furniture. On the stand beside the bed lay what looked to be a shriveled heart and internal parts Hannigan couldn't begin to identify or look at for more than a glimpse.

Sprawled on the bed lay the mutilated body of a woman, indescribable in the wanton butchery wrought upon it. She was unrecognizable, though her identity was not in doubt.

Gasping, he staggered back, unable to view the scene a moment longer. He shook his head in silent protest, barely conscious of sliding his gun into its holster and pressing his back to the opposite wall. Had that wall not been there he would have collapsed.

Tootie took the lantern from him before he dropped it. She stepped up to the threshold and peered inside, then quickly turned away, her face bleaching.

'Oh, sweet Jesus . . .' she muttered, then suddenly doubled over, vomiting to the side of the door. She retched for another moment but the sound barely penetrated his fragmented senses.

'I'm sorry, Jim . . .' he heard her say, after she had regained some of her composure. 'I'm so sorry.'

'Are you?' he muttered, a tear slipping from his eye. He whirled, emotion surging, and strode down the hall. Everything inside him wanted to run, get as far away from the ghastly sight as he could, but it was burned into his mind. The night air, warm and humid, made his senses swim even more. Inarticulate sounds came from his mouth as he staggered along the boardwalk into the darkness.

Tootie stumbled out of the boarding-house on shaky legs, her mind reeling from the horror in that room. She had no doubt who the body belonged to and great waves of sadness washed over her at the thought. Above that, her first concerns were for him, what he must have felt on finding Catherine that way; she felt no anger for his harsh words to her. She had a glimpse of understanding now why he worried so much over her on cases. What had happened to Catherine . . . the business they lived was no game, no reckless child's adventure. There were consequences and risks, deadly ones. He had wanted to protect her from this, and everything he might have ever feared was painted in scarlet in that room.

She paused on the boardwalk, struggling to hold her stomach down. Never had she seen anything like the death in that room. Those drawings Seckart made, they did no justice to what a butcher could do to a human body.

'God in Heaven . . .' she whispered, tears trickling from her eyes, making the kohl streak, the coral run. She'd been jealous of Catherine, maybe even envious over whatever she'd shared with Hannigan. But all she could feel now for her was a chasm of grief.

Gripping her composure as best she could, she peered along the boardwalk. She would follow him, comfort him, whether he accepted it or not.

Someone stepped from the shadows across the street. It took her only an instant to identify the man as the marshal. A peculiar look registered on his face, one she was too distraught to read. Knowing he had seen her, she started to yell out to him, to tell him about the murder. Before she got a word out, someone grabbed her from behind so hard and so fast the marshal likely couldn't even tell why she withdrew so swiftly into the shadows of the alley running beside the boarding-house.

She struggled, but a tremendous pressure jammed

against her throat. A forearm blocked her air. She kicked backward, trying to rake her assailant's shin, but the man was too powerful, had too good a grip on her and was taking no chances this time. Her senses started gyrating from the lack of oxygen. Fear sprang into her thoughts, the fear that Hannigan would find her the same way he'd found Catherine and that it would destroy him.

The thought didn't last for long, because blackness swept over her mind and swallowed her senses.

CHAPTER TEN

Jim Hannigan's mind wandered through old memories, memories now drenched in blood. He saw Catherine the way she looked those years ago, young, vital, unsoiled by the ravages of her profession. Then scarlet washed across the scenes in his mind, bringing suffocating waves of grief. He reached the end of town, stumbled out into the street. He dropped to his knees, overwhelmed by dark emotions, and threw back his head, screamed at the unfeeling sky. He shook his fists at the crescent moon, cursed at the cold stars. Tears flooded his eyes, and he could barely breathe as sobs shuddered through him.

She was dead. Butchered like the others. Worse. The killer had murdered her in a frenzy of blood and unholy fever. No one should have had to die that way; no one deserved her fate, even the lowliest outlaw.

It was his fault. He should have been there for her. He should have gone to her earlier, persuaded her to leave this town, just as he should have found a way to persuade Tootie.

Her name shook him from his useless sobs. The darkened street appeared before him, shimmering in his tear-flooded vision. He had said something to her she didn't deserve. Something he'd never be able to take back if the killer got to her first, and Hannigan was certain she would be the next target now that he had taken Catherine.

He rose to his feet. His legs were unsteady, but his mind was clearer now, focused on the woman who had come in with him. He would have to grieve later.

Where would she be? She wouldn't have returned to the saloon, not after what she'd said to the owner. The hotel, maybe, her room. He would look there, tell her to pack her bag and be ready to ride within an hour. No way he would let her stay in this town, now.

First, he would find Severin to inform him about Catherine, make arrangements for her funeral, and let the man know in no uncertain terms that he would return with the county marshal's men and turn over every rock in this god-forsaken hole until he found the man responsible for these heinous acts. The lawdog wouldn't like it, but Hannigan didn't give a damn.

He staggered onto the boardwalk, feet dragging, legs leaden. It was all he could to keep his thoughts from going back to that room of death.

Moments later, he reached the marshal's office and pushed open the door. Wall lanterns lit the office, barely warding off the shadows. Darkwolf looked up from where he sat on his bunk. He scowled. The marshal was nowhere to be seen. Scanning the room, Hannigan's gaze paused on a suitcase near the lawdog's desk, then skipped back to the Indian.

'Where's Severin?'

Darkwolf shrugged.

Hannigan left the office and headed for the hotel, wondering where the lawdog had gotten off to, but he

149

could find him later, after telling Tootie to get her gear together.

When he entered the hotel he froze. His gaze locked on to the form of the clerk, who lay sprawled over the counter. Hannigan's nerves tingled, a surge of dark dread washing over him. He went to the clerk, who lay face down, and turned him over. A gaping chasm yawned in the man's throat, ear to ear. Blood soaked the counter top.

'Christ . . . Tootie . . .' he whispered. His hand went to the Peacemaker and lifted it from its holster. He stared at the stairway leading to the upper level, as if it was a passageway to another glimpse of hell.

Throwing caution aside as the dread built into a panic, he ran to the stairs, taking them three at a time until he reached the top.

Peering down the hall, he saw immediately the door to his room stood open. His heart skipped, then pounded in his throat. He made his way down the hall, hand shaking again, legs unsteady.

'No . . .' he whispered, shaking his head. 'Please not her, too . . .'

Even before he reached his room, light from inside told him someone was in there – or had been.

Bracing himself against what he might see, he stepped around to the front of the opened door and stood in the threshold, gun leveled.

'Ah, you do not disappointment me,' the man inside said. He held Tootie in front of him, a knife jammed to her throat. Her make-up was smeared, her face battered, her bodice torn. Her eyelids fluttered as the man pressed his blade harder against the soft flesh of her throat.

Hannigan recognized the man instantly, though it had been years since he'd seen him.

'You . . .'

'Ah, Monsieur Hannigan, you remember your old friend Bertrand Mitre. Good, good. I hoped you would.'

'I remember. I put you away . . .' Hannigan took a single step into the room.

'Uh-uh.' Mitre pulled the knife away from Tootie's throat an inch, then brought it back in a threatening gesture. A misstep and the outlaw would draw it across her jugular. 'That is far enough, I think. Drop your gun.'

The manhunter hesitated. If he dropped the gun he would have no way of helping her, but if he didn't Mitre would slit her throat. 'Don't hurt her. If you want me, take me, but leave her alone.'

'I said drop your gun!' Mitre's voice snapped out and Hannigan let the Peacemaker fall to the floor. 'Kick it over against the wall.'

Hannigan booted the gun. It skidded over to the window.

'What do you want, Mitre?' The sight of the man confused Hannigan. Was this his killer?

'Want? I want you to pay for burying me in that hell-hole. I want you to suffer by watching your woman die before your eyes.'

Sweat trickled down Hannigan's brow. He saw little hope but to stall him. 'You weren't a killer, Mitre. It was simple robbery.'

The man laughed, and Hannigan knew he had no chance of talking this man out of what he intended. 'That's where you're wrong, Monsieur. I killed plenty and enjoyed each one. My knife, she has tasted more blood than your gun, I am certain. I only tell you this now because in another moment it won't matter.' Mitre dragged Tootie with him as he maneuvered towards where

Hannigan's gun lay. His intent was clear: he would cut Tootie's throat, drop her and grab the gun to end Hannigan's life.

The manhunter saw Tootie's head drop a fraction and a look flashed into her eyes. He wanted to shout no, stop her from what he realized she was about to do, but she was dead anyway if she didn't try.

He tensed, ready to leap, though he was sure it would not be in time.

Tootie let out a chopped yell as her fingers curled into a fist that snapped backward, burying itself in Mitre's crotch.

Mitre cursed and jerked the knife. Tootie dropped straight down but the blade caught the corner of her jaw and blood streamed. She hit the floor, rolled.

Hannigan leaped the moment Tootie made her move. Mitre, agony on his face, but panicked, made a grab for the gun. The manhunter slammed into him, propelled the outlaw backward into the window.

Glass shattered and Mitre tottered onward, going straight through. Hannigan grabbed him by the knife wrist and a handful of shirt, jerked him inward, then hurled him against the wall beside the window. The knife dropped from Mitre's hand and a stunned looked crossed his eyes. The look vanished and he tried to get his hands around Hannigan's throat.

Every ounce of rage in Hannigan's body surged. Flashes of Catherine's body, Tootie's brush with death, swept through his mind, driving him into a killing frenzy. He slammed Mitre into the wall again and again, battering the man into submission, then flinging him sideways over the bed. The outlaw hit the floor hard, but instantly struggled to get back to his feet.

The manhunter grabbed him by the back of the shirt and hoisted him up, flung him against the wall head first. Mitre hit with a resounding crash, by some quirk of fate not breaking his neck. He collapsed, groaning on the floor. Hannigan jumped atop him, began pounding Mitre's face into a bloody mess. He probably broke a knuckle but didn't feel anything other than an insane fury and need to make the outlaw pay for everything that had happened tonight. His fist came up for another blow, one that would likely end the outlaw's life.

A hand grabbed his upraised fist. Startled, he looked back to see Tootie, eyes pleading, blood dripping from her jaw.

'No, Jim. We need him to tell us if he killed those other women.'

Hannigan peered at her, uncomprehending for a moment, then relaxed his fist. He backed off Mitre, coming to his feet. The outlaw curled into a fetal position, groaning.

Hannigan grabbed Tootie, held her close. Her wound was superficial, but she had been lucky. He had been lucky. He hadn't lost her.

There came a sound from behind him and he drew back, his gaze going to the doorway. A man stood there, eyes lingering on the outlaw, then jumping to them.

'How'd you get here?' Hannigan asked, surprised to see the man standing in the doorway.

Marshal Severin held Hannigan's gaze, took a step into the room. 'I came to see you about the murder of the woman I saw you two with last night. The woman who owns the boarding house heard a commotion and found a body. She said she saw two people leaving the scene, described you both. When I got here I found the clerk dead and came on up looking for you.' Severin glanced at the outlaw again. 'Appears you caught your killer after all.'

Hannigan glanced at Mitre. 'Won't know that till I question him.'

The marshal nodded, then went over to the outlaw, gave him a kick. 'On your feet.' He grabbed the outlaw's arm, helping him up.

Mitre glared at Hannigan, blood pouring from his mouth. 'I'll get out again, Hannigan. What happened to those women won't be nothing compared to the way they'll find you. You mark my word.'

'I'll hold on to him till you question him, Hannigan,' the marshal said. 'I'll count on seeing you at first light.'

Hannigan nodded. The marshal led Mitre from the room. The manhunter looked at Tootie, struggling to find words, wanting to tell her how much she meant to him, that if he lost her he lost everything. Why was it so goddamn hard? Why couldn't he just tell her—

A sound from beyond the door cut off the thought. A bang, then the heavy thudding that Hannigan knew could only be a body tumbling down the steps.

Hannigan darted to the window, grabbed his Peacemaker, then dashed out into the hallway. He saw the marshal standing at the top of the stairs, a knife in his hand, dripping blood.

'He tried to grab my knife . . .' Severin stared down, not bothering to look at Hannigan.

Hannigan's gaze swept down the stairs. Mitre lay sprawled in a heap at the bottom. He went down, turned over the body. Mitre's throat was sliced, the cut deep enough to leave the outlaw's head canted at an unnatural angle.

'Christ, Severin, you nearly cut his head off.' Hannigan

watched Severin come down the steps and stop before the body.

The lawdog shrugged. 'Saves the town the cost of a trial.'

Hannigan peered at the lawdog, his dislike strengthening with something else he couldn't quite put a finger on. 'Maybe . . .'

'What is that supposed to mean?' Something came into the marshal's cold blue eyes. Hannigan wasn't sure what. His mind was still too entangled with all that had happened this night to think clearly.

'I'll see you in the morning,' he said, words low and promising something he couldn't bring to the surface.

Severin smiled, a dark expression. 'Go back to your room, Mr Hannigan. Think things over. Make sure your woman's safe, yes?' Severin laughed a low laugh, then walked away. He went to the body of the clerk, pulled it off the counter and dropped it on the floor. Hannigan gave Mitre a final glance then headed up the stairs.

Morning light blazed through the window of Jim Hannigan's hotel room. Another sleepless night filled with bloodstained images of Catherine and Mitre, of nearly losing Tootie again. He would welcome leaving this town. He never wanted to see it again.

His thoughts had also taken other roads, ones paved with suspicions with which he would soon confront the town's marshal.

A knock on his door told him Tootie was ready to go to the lawdog's office with him. He opened it, seeing her worn face and bloodshot eyes and knowing she hadn't slept, either. She had dressed in a cream blouse and riding-skirt. Her hair was straight and she wore no make-up.

She looked at the floor, then back to him. 'I know it doesn't mean much, Jim, but I thought about it all night. I'm sorry for what happened to her. I really am. I would never wish that on anyone.'

'I know . . .' he said, voice low. 'I . . .' Christ, he had never said he was sorry to anyone. It came a lot harder than it should have. 'I didn't mean what I said . . .' he managed to get out. It was the best he could do.

She nodded and they walked towards the stairs. 'Mitre, you knew him?'

'Put him away years ago for robbery. Apparently he held a grudge.'

'Why would he kill those women?' Her tone said she didn't believe the outlaw guilty, and neither did he.

'Reckon we both came to the same thought. He had no reason to kill those women. I reckon he was trailing us, watching us for a spell. We led him here, not the other way around.'

'Then the murderer?'

'Is still out there. But I got a funny feeling in my gut . . .'

'Who?' She peered at him as they reached the bottom of the stairs.

'Something I saw last night didn't sit well with me. Kept thinking something was wrong, but I couldn't figure what. Then it came to me early this morning. The way Mitre's throat was cut. Severin damn near took his head off, but Mitre didn't even cry out. I saw the same type of cut on that body at Francis's office.'

Shock flashed across on her face, but she remained silent until they reached the marshal's office.

Hannigan opened the door, his hand on his gun butt, keeping Tootie in back of him. If what he suspected was right, Severin would be dangerous when confronted, and if he were the killer Hannigan had already decided that the man wasn't walking out of this office.

He heard Tootie gasp as they stepped inside. The office was empty, but in the cell at the back a body lay sprawled across the bunk, throat cut from ear to ear. The head canted at an angle that showed Aaron Darkwolf had nearly been decapitated.

Hannigan's gaze went to the desk. The suitcase that had been there the night before was missing.

'I reckon that's a confession,' he whispered.

Jim Hannigan and Tootie del Pelado spent the next two weeks searching for any sign of Marshal Severin, but found no trace of the vanished lawdog. A passing stage found his suitcase, its contents sprawled about the ground. The territorial marshal concluded that the lawdog had been set upon by bandits or Indians and murdered.

No more brutal killings occurred in Miller's Pass.

EPILOGUE

Boston Harbor

A Cunard steamship, the *Servia*, loomed above the dock, a magnificent vessel, the first to be lit by electricity. Under a milky-gray sky it boarded passengers for its journey to London. Seagulls screeched in the air and the salt water carried an acrid scent difficult for George Severin to tolerate after so much time in the sweet-scented air of Colorado.

He stepped up to the purser at the base of the gangplank and handed him a ticket. The purser glanced at the ticket, then at Severin, who was dressed in a dark suit with a cutaway coat. He'd replaced the dark Stetson with a more conservative black felt hat.

'Where in London you headed, Mr Severin?' asked the purser, making conversation without much enthusiasm.

Severin gazed at him. 'I have business in Whitechapel.'

'Whitechapel?' The purser shook his head, passing him back his ticket. 'Never heard of it.'

Severin smiled, a dark little expression that crawled up from somewhere in the depths of his mind. 'Perhaps then I shall make it famous . . .'

He went up the gangplank, pausing half-way and fishing in a pocket of his suitcoat. He drew out a tin star, gazed at it with a soft laugh, then tossed it into the gray water below. 'Perhaps I will make it famous, indeed . . .'

EPILOGUE TWO

From the files of the Miller's Pass Ledger:

July, 1889:
Saloon-owner Jack Pruitt was found dead this morning, floating face down in a stream at the edge of town, a knife embedded in his back. A saloon girl is being held for questioning. The young woman claims the saloon owner was beating her and she killed him in self-defense. Trial set to begin Monday, but this reporter holds little doubt she will be exonerated.

October, 1892:
Doctor T. Francis, town physician, died last night from a long-term illness of an undisclosed nature. Apparently he had been suffering from the malady for many years and had searched in vain for a cure through the study of human organs.

February, 1897:
Newspaper owner Arthur Seckart was shot to death by his wife late last night. Apparently the altercation took place upon his wife's discovery of the man in a compromising situation with one of his local models. No charges have been filed, pending an investigation.

From the Pall Mall Gazette:

1903:
George Severin, a local constable convicted of poisoning his wife, was hanged for his crimes. It is suspected he dealt the same fate to previous women unfortunate enough to wed him.